Sea of tears

To Keith, whose dream is to live in Barbados

JANETTA OTTER-BARRY BOOKS

Sea of Tears copyright © Frances Lincoln Limited 2011
Text copyright © Floella Benjamin 2011
Cover illustration by David Dean

First published in Great Britain in 2011 and in the USA in 2012 by
Frances Lincoln Children's Books, 4 Torriano Mews,
Torriano Avenue, London NW5 2RZ
www.franceslincoln.com

A catalogue record for this book is available from the British Library.

ISBN 978-1-84780-058-9

Printed and bound by CPI Group (UK) Ltd, Croydon, CR0 4YY in August 2011

1 3 5 7 9 8 6 4 2

Sea of tears

FLOELLA BENJAMIN

F

FRANCES LINCOLN
CHILDREN'S BOOKS

Chapter One

Jasmine's eyes opened and scanned the bare walls of her room. Traces of Blu-tac stained the white wallpaper where her posters had been. The empty room felt like a prison cell. Only her bed and a small side-table remained – everything else had gone, even the carpet. It was horrible.

This was the room she had grown up in, her safe haven, the place where she felt happy and secure, the place she ran to when everything was going wrong. Now the shrill beeping of her alarm clock bounced harshly off the bare walls. And the clattering of her mother moving around downstairs was amplified by the emptiness of the house.

Jasmine pulled the duvet over her head and tried to force herself back to sleep but, perfectly on cue, came her mother's yell from the bottom of the stairs.

'Jazzie! It's six o'clock... time to get up. The taxi's here in an hour!'

Jasmine stayed silent. Why did her mother

always have to shout so loud?

'Jasmine!'

This time it was her real name. Her mum always did that... first the pretence at being nice with the Jazzie thing, then, when she started to get annoyed, it became Jasmine.

The floorboards felt cold and splintery as she padded across to the door, opening it just wide enough to shout back. 'I'm up... stop yelling.'

'Well, have a wash, get dressed and come down for breakfast. And don't be rude, young lady, and don't take liberties just because your dad's not here.... Show some respect.... Oh, and bring your bedclothes down with you.'

Jasmine went over to the window and pulled aside the old sheet that her mother had put up in place of her lovely, blue, flowery curtains, which were now, along with all her other possessions, on their way to Barbados.

It had been difficult deciding what to take and what to leave. Many arguments had taken place as to what was necessary and what wasn't. Jasmine had lost most of them of course. She had watched in despair as her precious old toys and winter clothes were given away to charity shops.

They were buying new furniture in Barbados, so their old furniture had been sold, given away or taken to the recycling centre. Everything else had been packed into large, blue plastic drums and wooden packing-cases to be transported in a container across the Atlantic by ship.

Jasmine's dad, who had flown out six months ago to prepare for their arrival, would have to get the container through the strict Customs in Barbados and get everything delivered to the house.

Jasmine had not seen the house, but already she hated the thought of it. Nothing could ever replace the affection she felt for her cosy, south London semi.

As the hazy morning sunlight burst in, she rubbed her eyes. They were still puffy and sore from all the crying she had done the night before. She felt a lump rise in her throat again as she remembered the tearful goodbyes with her three best friends.

It was the start of the school summer holidays, a time that would normally be for going out, a time for fun and laughter. But Rachel, Michaela and Sam had come over yesterday, and they had sat in the empty front room and basically just cried.

'It's gonna be so great... innit,' enthused Sam, trying to lift everyone's spirits in her usual, upbeat way. 'Barbados sounds so, like, cool. Will you be livin' on the beach under a palm tree?'

'Yea, wiv Reggae music playin' all the time,' added Michaela, curling one of her ringlets round her finger.

'Don't be stupid, that's Jamaica!' Rachel said crushingly.

Of course none of them had ever been out of south London, and the only images they had seen of the Caribbean were on adverts for fruity drinks on the TV.

They had all promised to come out to Barbados and see her, but Jasmine knew deep in her heart there was little chance of that. She realised that, in reality, this was probably the last time she would see her friends, and it hurt so badly she wanted to scream with frustration and anger at what her parents were doing to her.

She stared out at the familiar street, where she had walked so many times. The rubbish truck was making its noisy way up the road, the bin men banging and crashing the wheelie bins, oblivious to people asleep in the houses. The truck snorted its way up to the gate below, and one of the men rolled the overflowing bin up to its gaping chasm. The truck's two metal claws grabbed it, and the contents lurched into the crushers.

In went the last remaining bits and pieces of Jasmine's life at Number 73, Cromer Road, SE26. The old, broken lamp that had lit so many bedtime stories while her dad sat in its warm glow; the bag of old magazines that had accumulated under her bed; the faded, cardboard cut-out of Beyonce that had hung on the back of her bedroom door for the last five years. The crusher made short work of them all, and the man carelessly rattled the bin back on to the pavement and swiftly moved on.

Jasmine let go of the sheet, turned away from the window and headed for the bathroom with a sick, empty feeling in her stomach.

The mirror was still on the wall above the sink. Part of the 'fixtures and fittings', Dad had said. She wished she could smash it and stop it showing her puffy, tear-stained face staring back at her.

To make matters worse, a new spot had erupted during the night and it stood out yellow and tight on her forehead, as if to say, 'Ha ha, hello there, I'm here just to make you even more miserable.' Jasmine viciously squeezed it, and its contents splattered on the mirror, leaving a globule of watery blood on her brown skin.

The hot-water heater had been switched off, and the cold splash felt strangely comforting as Jasmine half-heartedly washed and brushed her teeth. She dragged on her jeans and the 'Friends for Eternity' T-shirt Michaela had given her as a going-away present.

She took one final look round her empty bedroom, then silently closed the door behind her and reluctantly made her way down the stairs, at the bottom of which were the suitcases packed with clothes and essentials for the flight. She felt like kicking them but resisted the urge.

In the kitchen Jasmine's mother was frantically wiping surfaces with a handful of kitchen roll. On the worktop next to the hob, a paper plate with a slice of toast on it sat forlornly next to a plastic cup full of orange juice.

'Quickly – eat your breakfast,' said her mum. 'I want to wipe that top off before we go.'

'Why are you cleaning everything, Mum? We don't live here any more.'

'Listen, I don't want the Framptons thinking we are dirty people. Now, less of the backchat and eat up.'

The Framptons were the young couple who had bought the house and would be moving in later that day. Mum and Dad had been in the house for over twenty years and it was the only home Jasmine had ever known. It was a typical, terraced, south-London house dating back to Victorian times. Dad had done most of the decorating, and kept embarrassingly announcing to everyone that he had bought it for thirty thousand pounds and got over ten times more than he had paid for it when they sold it.

The house had ornate, plaster cornices on the ceilings and in the front room there was the original fireplace, something everyone seemed to get very excited about. Jasmine couldn't see the point of a fireplace herself – no one had ever lit a fire in it.

But at Christmas-time her mother decorated it with holly and pine branches, and on Christmas Eve she would put a sip of sherry and a carrot above the fireplace and hang out a big red stocking for Santa to put her presents in. Jasmine had figured out that Santa didn't really come down the chimney, or even exist, when she was about six. But she never said anything as she didn't want to upset her mother, who seemed to get so much pleasure out of doing it.

She wondered if the new house would have

a fireplace... or if they even celebrated Christmas in Barbados. Father Christmas and his sleigh pulled by reindeer seemed a bit out of place on a palm-fringed beach.

'Stop day-dreaming and finish your breakfast!' Her mother's voice burst into her thoughts, snapping her back to reality. 'The taxi will be here soon so get your stuff together...now!'

Jasmine just about managed to force down the soggy toast. Then she finished her juice, put the cup into a bag with the rest of the final rubbish and sullenly took the bag outside. She dropped it with a thud into the empty wheelie bin which the dustbin men had, as usual, left blocking the pavement.

She looked up and down the street. It gave her a strange, melancholy feeling. This had always been 'her street', the street where she had played 'Don't step on the paving-stone lines' on the way back from school or rushing home to see her favourite television programme. A familiar place where she had learnt to ride her bike, where she had fallen over a dozen times as she tried to master skateboarding and rollerblading. Now it was just another street amongst the thousands criss-crossing London's suburban sprawl.

As Jasmine stood there, a blue people-carrier

came slowly up the road, its driver craning his neck to see the house numbers. It stopped opposite, in Mr Cranbourne's disabled parking space – which was the only possible place to stop without causing a traffic jam. It didn't really matter because Mr Cranbourne, who had one leg, didn't have a car, and every other inch of the streets in every direction was lined with so many cars it was impossible to park. The driver tooted at Jasmine and pointed at his watch.

'Taxi's here!' Jasmine shouted through the open front door.

'Well, come and get the cases, for Goodness' sake, instead of standing there with your two long hands... what's wrong with you this morning, girl? You're in another world."

Jasmine stood by the two cases in the hallway, her heart beating faster, her hands clenched tightly. She swallowed hard but the lump in her throat seemed to grow larger as her eyes filled with tears. Suddenly her knees weakened and she felt herself crumpling to the floor as if she were about to pray.

At that moment her mother came bustling out of the kitchen, fumbling in her handbag. 'Oh dear... where did I put the keys? I have to leave them next door with Mrs Lehman....'

Jasmine was on her knees, sobbing silently. Her mother looked down, shocked and surprised.

'Oh, Jazzie darlin'...what is it?' she said, dropping down beside Jasmine, cradling her in her arms as she used to when Jasmine was a child and had fallen over and hurt herself. 'Tell me what's the matter, Jazzie. What is it?'

Jasmine's tears had now become deep and uncontrollable, her body shaking violently with each sob.

'I don't want... to leave... the house....' she gasped.

'Oh, Jazzie,' sighed her mother. 'I've been so busy with the move, I didn't realise....'

'You and Dad just don't understand... it's so unfair! I love everything about this house. I'm happy here.'

Her mother took a tissue out of her bag and carefully wiped away Jasmine's tears. 'I feel the same way too, Jazzie. This is where your dad and I came when we got married, it's where you were born. Yes, it has so many happy memories for me too.' Suddenly her mother's eyes took on a distant look and a tear rolled down her cheek. 'And sad ones as well.... Remember when we lost little Jason that night in his sleep?'

Jasmine's heart missed a beat at the mention of the little brother she had lost, and the terrible grief she had felt. She had been so happy to have a baby brother to look after. But he had died one November night, aged only five months, a victim of cot death. Yes, the house held sad memories too, she thought. But some of the pain had eased over the last seven years.

'You were so brave then, and having you to love made it easier for your dad and me. But now it's time to move on,' said her mother softly.

'Why?' sniffed Jasmine.

'Jazzie, we've been through all this....'

Outside, the taxi driver was impatiently tooting his horn.

'Come on, Jazzie darlin', get up and let's say goodbye to the house together,' said her mum, forcing herself to smile.

Jasmine knew it was hopeless. She could never win, there was no way she could change the situation. So she sniffed away the last of her tears and stood up, pulling herself together before she dragged the suitcases over to the taxi. Meanwhile her mother locked up and shoved the keys through the next-door neighbour's letter-box. Then they stood silently by their front gate, arms round each other's shoulders, gazing sadly up at the curtainless windows, both knowing this was the last time they would see the house.

'Bye, house,' whispered Jasmine.

'Thanks for everything,' added her mother.

From the taxi, Jasmine took one last look along the street. Then she turned and stared through the windscreen as the driver accelerated away towards the airport and her new life, thousands of miles from the drab streets of south London, far from the grey skies of Britain.

Chapter Two

As the cab weaved in and out of the early morning traffic, Jasmine thought back to the events of the last year.

It had been the most unhappy few months of her life, and the turbulent events that had brought her to this day flashed through her brain like a wild dream. She remembered the day when she came home from school and her life fell apart. She closed her eyes and replayed the scene when her parents announced the momentous decision they had made. A decision they had made without consulting her.

It was over a year ago, and Jasmine was standing in the corridor outside her form-room at Jibson School. The last stragglers were lazily making their way to their various rooms and Mr Hobson, the Deputy Head, stalked the corridors, pouncing on latecomers like a overgrown pit bull.

Jasmine dodged into the classroom, sat at her desk and looked round at the familiar faces of her classmates. Miss Vine, the form teacher, was still in the staff room so everyone was gathered in small groups, talking animatedly about the usual mixture of gossip and scandal.

The big news was that Dave Groves, a boy in their year, had been excluded for bringing a screwdriver to school and threatening to stab Leon Akuba with it. There was always trouble between the two of them. Leon kept calling Groves a 'Reggae Boy' because of his locks. Leon's parents were from Ghana, and he was always going on about being a real African, not a slave boy like Groves.

Michaela, Jasmine's best friend, hurried over, her mass of brown ringlets bouncing round her smiling face. 'Hi Jazzie, what's happ'nin'?'

'Nuttin' much,' replied Jasmine, giving her a quick hug.

Just then the door swung open and in bustled Miss Vine, carrying a pile of books. 'Right, everyone, take a seat and let's get on with it.'

Jasmine really liked Miss Vine. She was young, in her mid twenties, with long blonde hair held back with an Alice band, and she always had a ready smile. She was from a posh background, a real English rose, and though she tried hard to cover her accent everyone called her Princess Di. She usually wore a pink or blue cotton shirt with the collar turned up, and had a string of pearls decorating her neck.

She also took hockey, and was more like one of the girls than a teacher. Being a First Year was made easier for Jasmine because of Miss Vine. She gave her confidence and was always there to listen if she had a problem.

'Is Dave going to go to prison, Miss?' shouted somebody.

'I suggest we forget about that unfortunate incident and concentrate on our lessons,' replied Miss Vine. She had a way of keeping the class under control without being strict or shouting at them.

Yes, the feeling among the whole class was that she truly was more like a friend than a teacher, and they respected her.

The day ended with a walk through the local shopping centre. Jasmine, Sam, Michaela and Rachel shrieked with laughter as they avoided the attentions of a gang of boys from Langford Park School, who had stuffed their blazers into their rucksacks and donned hoodies and baseball caps.

The boys strutted noisily past elderly, nervous shoppers, making signs at the surveillance cameras they knew were watching them. Jasmine thought they were stupid, giving young people a bad name.

The shops were always full of exciting things, designer stuff, and the shop assistants eyed Jasmine and her friends suspiciously as they handled expensive items which four 12-year-old schoolgirls patently could not afford.

Rachel's brother had been caught shoplifting. He had gone to the shopping centre with some other boys who had got caught taking something, and because he was with them he had been implicated as well, even though he had not taken anything.

Jasmine's mother kept going on about this, and told her to stay away from the shopping centre. Jasmine often went there after school without telling her, but she didn't hang around there for too long in case her mum found out.

❖ ❖ ❖

Generally speaking, life was OK for Jasmine, although she sometimes wished people would see her as a person, not as a colour. When she was little she hadn't thought too much about it, but gradually she began to notice things people said and the way they looked at her.

When she went to her first school the kids seemed to polarise into two groups, black and white, even though the teachers made strenuous efforts to mix them up.

She remembered the first time someone called her a name. She was just six. She had met her mother at the gate and burst into tears. 'I don't like being black. People say horrible things and make fun of me!' she sobbed.

'Listen, Jazzie,' said her mother, hugging her tightly. 'Some people won't like you because of your brown skin. But remember your mummy and your daddy love you, and you must love yourself, because you're special and always will be.'

But she could see her mother was really upset, even though she tried to be positive.

As Jasmine grew older she learned how to deal with it, but most of her friends were black or, like Michaela, mixed-race.

Mind you, it wasn't just a case of black and white. The Somali kids were always fighting with the

Eritreans and the Indian kids with the Pakistani ones. The Muslim girls with their head-scarves tended to stick together, but occasionally things came to a head and trouble broke out. Mr Turnbull, the Head, was always speaking to parents and trying to smooth things over, but it was a thankless task and some days the strain showed on his normally smiling face.

Jasmine had been at the school just under three months, and she and everybody else in her class were already looking forward to the prospect of moving up into Year 8. As a First Year you always felt as if you were the lowest of the low - at least when you got into the second year you had someone to look down on.

The other exciting thing was boys. For the first time, Jasmine and her friends started to take an interest in them. Sure, they were idiots and acted stupid most of the time, but one or two of them looked as if they might be of interest. Of course Jasmine's mum and dad were dead against anything like that. They wanted to keep her tied to her books, studying continuously.

'If you want to get on in this world you need to have an education!' her dad would preach. 'You won't be able to just waltz into a job.'

'Yes, if you're white you're all right, but if you're black, stand back, unless you have an education,' her mum would say. 'That's what my mother used to say to me, God rest her soul.'

So boys were definitely a no-no with her parents.

❖ ❖ ❖

One Saturday, everyone was invited to Simon Kerplinski's house for his birthday party. He proudly announced on the invititation that his parents would not be there.

'You're not going!' her mother said straight away, with a note of finality in her voice.

'Oh, please,' begged Jasmine. 'Everybody else is going.'

'Well, you're not everyone,' retorted Mum. 'What kind of parents are they, leaving a bunch of 12-year-olds to run riot? It sounds like a recipe for disaster.'

'Let her go,' interrupted Dad, playing the good cop for a change. 'I'll drive her there and pick her up if it makes you feel any better.'

Eventually Mum had reluctantly agreed.

On the night of the party, Jasmine put on the new dress she had bought with Michaela, but not too much make-up, as Mum wouldn't have allowed that. Anyway, she could always put on more when she got to the party…

Dad dropped her off, as promised. 'Have a good time!' he shouted out of the car window. 'Give me a call when you want me to pick you up.'

'OK, I will,' hissed Jasmine, praying that none of her friends had seen her dad. However, as she crossed the road she did notice two or three other parents doing exactly the same thing. So she didn't feel too embarrassed, but she still wished they would give her and her friends a bit more freedom.

At first things went well. Simon Kerplinski's small, terraced house soon filled up with people, mostly from school but with a smattering of Polish cousins and friends from the football team he played for at weekends.

Jasmine squeezed into the kitchen where Michaela and Rachel were talking to two boys. They were both wearing Arsenal football shirts and baggy jeans.

'Hi, Jazzie,' screamed Michaela. 'This is Pete and Tony, they're footballers, aren't you?'

The boys tried to look cool. 'Yeah,' said Tony, 'I've got a trial for United next month.'

'Awesome,' said Jasmine.

'So you'll be rich soon,' giggled Rachel excitedly.

'Yeah, and you can be my Wag,' said Tony, putting

his arm round her.

'I'll get us some drinks,' said Pete, 'orange juice or Coke is all they've got.'

'Orange, please,' chorused the girls.

Pete went over to the kitchen table where the drinks were. He looked around furtively, before reaching into his jacket pocket and pulling out a small bottle of vodka. He poured some of the alcohol into each of the paper cups of orange juice, then carried them back to the giggling girls.

'Here you go, ladies,' he said, winking at Tony.

Jasmine was thirsty and she quickly emptied the cup. It tasted a bit funny but everyone else seemed to be drinking it. After a few minutes she began to feel a bit strange. The kitchen seemed to be getting hotter and she felt light-headed. Michaela and Rachel seemed besotted by Tony and Pete, so Jasmine decided to have a look round.

She stood in the hallway, looking into the front room where the music was pounding loudly out of Simon's dad's stereo, and twenty or so people were shuffling rhythmically to the beat. Over the din the doorbell rang, and without thinking she opened the door.

Five boys stood grinning on the step. They looked

older than the other partygoers, and bigger. 'We're friends of Bernie's,' one of them announced. 'He said we could come along.'

'Who's Bernie?' said Jasmine.

'Never mind, he said it would be OK,' said another one, pushing his way past Jasmine. The others pushed past too and made straight for the kitchen.

Jasmine closed the front door, feeling a little worried about what she had just done. Within a minute or two all hell broke loose. Screams and shouts came from the kitchen area and people came rushing out. The sound of breaking glass and crockery was followed by more screams. Tony, his face covered in blood, staggered towards the hallway. Behind him Jasmine could see flailing fists and feet. People started to run past her and out of the front door.

Michaela came up the hallway looking unsteady on her feet.

'What's going on, Miki?'

Michaela didn't answer. She was leaning against the wall, her eyes half closed.

Rachel arrived, and she also looked very unsteady on her feet. 'Get outside!' she yelled, pulling Jasmine and Michaela out of the door and along the garden path. Just as they reached the gate, an upstairs window exploded outwards and shards of glass showered on to the lawn.

'What's happening?' screamed Jasmine, as they huddled together, her head still spinning from the effects of the vodka.

'Those boys that just arrived, they weren't invited, they were gatecrashers and they started a fight with Tony and Pete. It was horrible,' slurred Rachel.

'I'm calling my dad,' said Jasmine, fumbling for her mobile in her glittery handbag.

As she dialled the number, the next-door neighbour came out. She was an oldish Indian lady, wearing a dressing gown. 'I've called the police!' she screeched. 'You kids are a disgrace.'

'Dad, come and get me. I don't like it here, there's a fight,' Jasmine cried into the phone.

'I'll be there in five minutes. Stay where you are,' came his reply.

A second later the gatecrashers tumbled out of the house. Three of them turned right, ran across the garden, jumped over the low hedge and disappeared up the street, yelling swear-words. The other two went in the opposite direction, between the garage door and Simon Kerplinski's dad's car. As they ran past, one of them picked up a brick and hurled it at the car, smashing its windscreen.

At the same moment Simon Kerplinski came out of the front door. 'Oh no, my dad's gonna go mad!' he groaned. 'He's gonna kill me!'

Just then a police car came speeding up the road, its siren blaring. It screeched to a halt outside, and two policemen got out. 'What the heck's going on?' one of them demanded.

'Older boys... gatecrashers. They ran off,' said Simon pathetically.

'Which way?'

Everyone pointed in different directions.

The policeman shook his head. 'Kids!' he said.

Jasmine's dad arrived a couple of minutes later to find twenty or so kids standing shivering in the street. Two more police cars had arrived by now and the area looked like a major crime scene.

'What the hell has happened?' he said, looking round. 'I thought it was just supposed to be a birthday party! You three, get in the car.'

As he drove them all home, Rachel was sick in the car. It smelt terrible for days.

Of course Mum found it impossible to resist making the most of the incident for weeks afterwards. She just wouldn't let it lie. 'I knew something like this would happen,' she crowed. 'Drinking, fighting... I wouldn't be surprised if there weren't drugs there as well. I don't know what this country is coming to. I should never have let you go, you could have been knifed!'

'Oh, Mum, no one had a knife!' protested Jasmine.

'How do you know? All these hoodie types carry knives nowadays. Don't you read the papers?'

Chapter Three

A few weeks later, something far more serious happened. It shook everyone and left Jasmine and her friends feeling shocked and frightened.

Cecile Williams was a shy, geeky girl who no one took too much notice of. She didn't have any friends and tended to keep herself to herself, spending most of her time in the library, on the computer. Her parents were quite well-off and her dad was away a lot of the time.

It happened during half-term. Jasmine glanced at the television in the kitchen and was confronted with a picture of Cecile.

'Mum... Mum... look, it's a girl from my school. What's she doing on the television?'

'Maybe she's won a competition or something,' said Mum, grabbing the remote and pressing the volume button.

The announcer's voice was saying that anyone with information on Cecile's whereabouts should ring this number. The picture then changed to a shot of football.... 'And now for sport,' the announcer went on.

Just then the phone rang. It was Michaela's mother.

'Oh, no!' gasped Jasmine's mum into the phone. 'How long?'

'What is it?' hissed Jasmine.

'Cecile Williams has gone missing,' whispered Mum, covering the phone.

Jasmine rushed up to her room and got straight online. The site was buzzing with messages.

It turned out that Cecile had left home the day before, saying she was meeting a friend at the shopping centre and had not been seen since. No one seemed to know much about her, or who this 'friend' was. The police were frantically trying to find her, and had already visited half the people in the class.

Sure enough, about half an hour later the doorbell rang. Jasmine looked through the curtains and saw a police car outside.

Mum's voice came up the stairs. 'Jazzie, the policeman wants a word with you.'

In the front room stood a policewoman and a man in plain clothes. 'Hello, Jasmine,' said the man. 'I'm

Sergeant Boateng and this is WPC Taylor. I expect you've heard about Cecile Williams going missing?'

Jasmine nodded.

'Have you spoken to her recently? We need to find out her movements. Can you help?'

'I hardly know her, she doesn't speak to me much.'

'Who does she speak to?' chipped in WPC Taylor.

'No one. She spends all her time on Facebook – she sometimes joins in a chat with us.'

'Has she been on recently?'

Jasmine shook her head, feeling a little guilty that she had never bothered to answer any of Cecile's messages.

'Well, thanks. Let us know if you hear anything,' smiled Seargeant Boateng as he made for the door.

'What do you think has happened to her?' asked Mum worriedly.

'Too early to say, but most of these things turn out to be nothing at all. She'll probably show up in a few hours.'

Jasmine could tell he was lying, and that he and WPC Taylor were very worried.

Later that day the news carried the story again and this time Jasmine and her Mum watched, with increasing amazement and concern.

Police were looking at CCTV pictures and had spotted Cecile talking to a man in the shopping centre. She was carrying a rucksack and wearing jeans and a denim jacket. The fuzzy picture showed her walking off towards the exit with the man!

By now all hell was breaking loose and Jasmine was on the phone or online constantly. Rumours began to spread, and some people's imaginations started to get the better of them. Someone even suggested she had been abducted by aliens.

The television in the kitchen was constantly tuned to the news channels and Mum would channel-hop to watch each news bulletin's version of the story, while speaking on the phone with other concerned parents.

Jasmine's mum was a leading light in the local Neighborhood Watch and considered herself a bit of a local authority on the crime scene in the area. But this was way out of her experience, and Jasmine could tell she was just as shocked as all the other parents about the disappearance of Cecile.

That evening it was revealed on the news that the police had looked on Cecile's computer and discovered she had been talking to a man on the internet. They now believed he was the man in the CCTV pictures, and that Cecile had gone off with him.

'Jasmine, have you been talking to any strange men on the internet?' asked her mum at the dinner table that night, a note of panic in her voice.

'Doh... do I look stupid?'

'Jasmine, I'm serious. You wouldn't do anything like that, would you? There are so many wicked people out there. God knows what her parents are going through.'

Suddenly the tears began to run down her face, and she snatched a handful of kitchen roll to soak them up.

'Mum, don't cry, they'll find her...' Jasmine was shocked by her mother's sudden tears.

Just then Dad came home from his kitchen-building job. His face looked tired and was still covered in a fine, white, powdery sawdust. He sat down heavily at the table, understanding straight away what was going on.

He threw down a copy of the local paper. 'This is a bad business,' he muttered, pointing to the large photo of Cecile which filled the front page. 'I hope you're not thinking of doing this, young lady,' he said, tapping the picture with his finger.

'Daaaad,' groaned Jasmine, 'I've told Mum I'm not stupid.... I don't talk to strange men online. Cecile's a geek... a nerd... a loser....'

'Now there's no need to talk about her like that. Goodness knows what's happened to her.' Mum was starting to cry again.

Dad put his arm around her. 'They'll find her, it's just a matter of time....'

That night the house was restless. Jasmine could hear her mum and dad talking in their bedroom... she couldn't sleep, anyway. She was feeling guilty about what she had said about Cecile, and she tried to imagine what her parents were going through. What was she thinking of, going off with a stranger like that? The school had only recently had a visit from the police, warning everyone about the dangers of the internet.

When Jasmine finally got off to sleep, light was already filtering though the curtains, and she was grateful there was no school in the morning.

The next thing she heard was her mother yelling at the top of her voice from the bottom of the stairs. 'They've found her! They've found her! Jazzie, come down, they've found her, thank the Lord.'

Jasmine was halfway down the stairs before she was fully awake.

The news was blaring from the TV in the kitchen. *Cecile Williams, the young girl who went missing three days ago after apparently meeting with a man she met on an internet chat-room, has been found safe and well in Bournemouth. A thirty-seven-year-old man has been arrested.*

'Thirty-seven! What the heck is he doing with a twelve-year-old girl? Mum was almost shouting at the TV. 'I hope they put him away for life!'

Just then the phone rang. It was Dad. Jasmine slid back upstairs and got on the phone to Michaela. 'Did you hear? They found her with some sleazebag old bloke.... My parents have been going spare - they think we're all online to perverts 24/7.'

'Mine too,' said Michaela. 'They won't let me go online without checking, it's a real drag.'

'Yeah, it's not as though we would do anything as dumb as her, is it?'

Chapter Four

The next time Jasmine asked to go out during the half-term holidays, the incident with Cecile was the first thing her mum brought up. 'Hope you're not going to meet anybody I don't know?'

'No, Mum, it's just a shopping trip with Sam and Michaela.'

Jasmine loved the excitement of going shopping without her parents. Especially as Dad always wanted to hold her hand in the shopping centre, where she was likely to be seen by all her friends.

'You're still my little girl,' he would say. But it was SO embarrassing.

Jasmine and her friends had a brilliant time that afternoon. They had gone to have a burger and met up with a gang of other kids from school and had a real laugh.

She was still smiling when she turned into Cromer Road and pushed open the gate to number 73.

But she knew immediately something was going

on, as soon as she slammed the front door behind her. Normally the house was silent and empty, as her parents would be still at work. But today the TV was on and both her parents were in the kitchen.

Mum was sitting at the table, and Dad was pacing nervously around, trying to look busy.

'Hello, Jazzie,' her mum smiled. 'Would you like a snack?'

Jasmine didn't like the look of this. Why was Mum home so early from the bank she worked in? And Dad was never usually home before 7pm.

'What's going on?' asked Jasmine suspiciously.

Mum let out a little laugh. Jasmine knew that laugh – Mum always did it when she was nervous.

'Nothing is going on, darlin', it's just that we have something to tell you... it's exciting news.'

'Oh my God, you're not pregnant are you?' Vivid flashes of a new baby exploded in Jasmine's head. The memory of Jason was still raw even though he had died six years ago.

'No, Mum's not pregnant,' Dad said, pain slicing across his face too. 'It's big news. Sit down and we'll tell you.'

Jasmine reluctantly sat down. 'Go on then, what is it?'

'We've decided to move, Jazzie.... We've been thinking about it for some time and -'

'Move... move? Where to? What's wrong with this house, it's near school, and work for you....'

'We know, Jazzie. But we've decided to move back home, to Barbados.'

The words hit her like a baseball bat. Her senses reeled and her mouth dropped open in utter disbelief. 'Barbados! Bloody Hell, are you kidding me?'

'You see, that's exactly what I mean,' exclaimed her mother. 'Jasmine, don't be so rude. Do not use language like that in this house. Get to your room.'

Jasmine felt the tears welling up in her eyes.

'That's why we are moving back!' continued her mother, as if Jasmine had already left the room.

Jasmine spun on her heels and ran up to her room, savagely slamming the door behind her. Two minutes later she was on the phone to Michaela, phone in one hand, the other on the computer to Sam on MSN.

'It's so unfair...' she sobbed. 'They can't do this to me.'

Dad's soft knocking interrupted her conversation. 'Jazzie?'

'I'll call you back,' she whispered. 'My dad's outside.'

'Can I come in, Jazzie?' said Dad.

'What is it?' she sniffed.

Dad pushed the door open slowly and edged into the room. He sat down gingerly on the bed. 'Jazzie....'

Jasmine stared at the wall on which a poster of Beyonce hung by a single blob of Blu-tac. She adored looking up at Beyonce. She was her heroine and she hoped that one day she could be like her. But that was going to be impossible if she was stuck in Barbados.

'Jazzie,' Dad repeated. 'Listen to me. I know it's come as a shock, but your mother and I have talked it over and over for a long time now. It'll be good for all of us.'

'Oh yeah... how will it be good for me? All my friends are here. I like it here. It's not about what I want, it's about what you and Mum want... you don't care if it makes me unhappy. It's all right for Mum - since Gran died last year she hasn't got any family, so I suppose you both feel you can move wherever you like. But what about me?'

It was true that Marcia had been born in south London and had lived there all her life. Her parents had arrived in England in the late 1960s, her mum from Jamaica and her dad from St Lucia. They had met on the ship, fallen in love and married a year later. Although her mother was a qualified teacher and her dad had been in the St Lucian police, they had struggled to make a life for themselves in a cold, unwelcoming London.

They had been told the streets of London were paved with gold, but they soon found out the harsh reality of life in Britain. Her mother had ended up working in a laundry and her dad became a bus conductor. Marcia had been brought up by them in the strict West Indian way and she expected the same standards of behaviour from Jasmine.

Her dad had passed away two years before and her mum had died unexpectedly from cancer only eleven months ago. Now she had no reason to stay in London or even in England.

'Of course we care. That's why we're doing it, to let you grow up in a better environment. Away from all this...' said Dad, swinging his arm in an all-encompassing arc.

'All what?' spat Jasmine.

'The danger, the violence, the nastiness....' Mum's voice wailed as she pushed open the bedroom door. She had crept up the stairs and had been standing outside Jasmine's room, listening. 'I can't stand living here any more, it's not the London I grew up in.'

'Your mother's right, Jazzie,' Dad said, glancing at his wife. 'South London's getting rough.'

'What are you two talking about?' Jasmine gasped, shaking her head in disbelief. 'I like south London. I can take care of myself, I'm streetwise.'

'We know, darlin', but back home in Barbados you will be a lot happier, and we will have a better quality of life....'

'It's your home, not mine.'

'Just think, you will be able to go to the beach at weekends,' said Dad, trying to ignore her hurtful comments. He so much wanted her to feel just as Caribbean as he did, and to celebrate that part of her heritage.

'The sun shines all the time. Well, almost,' smiled Mum weakly.

'I don't care about the beach and the sun, I don't care about primitive Caribbean life. I want to grow up here, where all my friends are and my school is. I don't want to go to some sleepy little desert island where nothing happens.'

'That's enough, young lady, don't be rude,' snapped Mum, looking over at her husband, knowing that what Jasmine had said would have hurt him.

'Barbados is not primitive.'

'Well it's been decided, Jazzie,' Dad said determinedly. 'This house is on the market and I'm going back to Barbados to renovate Summerland House. You'll love the old house. Your room's much bigger than this one.'

Summerland House was the house that Dad's family had owned for generations. It had been left to his mother, Grannie Braithwaite, and her four sisters. But now Dad's four great-aunts had died, and his mother had agreed to let him do it up and live there.

'I don't care,' shouted Jasmine.

'Well, you going to have to get used to the idea, it's all settled. We leave as soon as you break up for your summer holidays and you'll start school in Barbados next September, end of story!'

Dad stood up and left her room, shoulders down but with a sense of finality.

Her mother grimaced at Jasmine and went after him. 'Well, that went well,' she whispered sarcastically as she followed him into the kitchen.

'She'll get used to it,' said Dad. 'Give her three weeks in Barbados and she'll wonder what the heck she saw in this place.'

But upstairs Jasmine buried her head in her pillow

and sobbed.

So that was it, she thought, all decided and there was nothing she could do about it. Her life was being turned upside-down because of a decision made by her parents, and they had not even consulted her.

Chapter Five

That night Jasmine lay awake, thinking about how her life was being ruined. When the first watery glimmer of sunlight crept into her room, she finally fell into a deep slumber that was quickly shattered by the buzzing of her alarm clock.

The first thing thought that flashed into her brain was, 'They're not going to do this to me.'

This kept repeating itself over and over as she sluggishly washed and dragged on her school clothes. She ate breakfast quickly, avoiding the stare of her mother.

'Everything all right, darlin'?' Mum kept asking. She said it in a hopeful way, because it was very obvious that, as far as Jasmine was concerned, everything was far from all right.

Jasmine just grunted non-committally and carried on shovelling Rice Krispies into her mouth.

It was a cold, bright, winter day, and the trees stood like skeletons along Cromer Road, baring their branches to the icy blast.

As usual, Jasmine walked to the tram stop with her mother. But she ignored her mum's outstretched hand and pretended to fumble with her school bag.

As she got on the tram, the usual goodbye kiss was avoided and Jasmine noticed the hurt look in her mother's eyes as she muttered a sullen 'Bye'.

As soon as she arrived in class, Michaela, Sam and Rachel rushed over and hugged her tearfully.

'I can't believe they're doing this to you, Jazzie,' Sam said angrily.

Rachel's face lit up as she decided she had solved the problem. 'Tell them you don't want to go, they'll change their minds...'

'Rachel, they're selling the house, stupid, they won't change their minds,' snapped Michaela.

Rachel looked hurt. She was such a simple soul, trusting and kind, but not quick to grasp complex issues.

Michaela on the other hand understood only too well that this was a serious matter, that it looked inevitable that Jasmine was going, and there was very little that could be done about it.

'We'll come and visit you, it'll be cool...' said Sam, trying to look cheerful.

Germaine Dobson, all thirteen stone of her, broke away from her clique and sauntered over, a gleeful look on her large, pink face. 'Going back to where you came from, I hear....good riddance, I say.'

'You shut your fat face,' hissed Michaela, stepping protectively between her and Jasmine.

'Or what?' smirked Dobson.

Jasmine, who had been trying to hold back her emotions, suddenly let out a sob. She picked up her bag and ran towards the door, only to crash head-on with Miss Vine, who dropped the huge pile of books she was carrying.

'What on earth is going on?' she shouted at Jasmine's back, as she rapidly disappeared along the corridor and out into the playground.

'Will someone please tell me what has upset Jasmine Braithwaite?'

Jasmine continued to stumble out of the school gates, pushing past a few latecomers. Her run slowed to an aimless walk, tears still blurring her vision. 'They can't do this to me!' still rang in her ears.

When she reached the corner shop she sat down on the bench outside and pulled a tissue from her bag.

That morning she had stuffed her trainers, a pair

of jeans and a hooded jacket into the bag as well. She didn't know why, she just wasn't thinking straight. She felt angry and powerless and those words just kept going round and round in her head. 'They can't do this to me.'

She had never bunked off school in her life but now she just didn't want to go back.

It was obvious the news of her move to Barbados had spread like wildfire on Facebook and the gossip machine was in overdrive. Germaine Dobson and her crew wouldn't let something as juicy as this go. Jasmine had never understood why Germaine hated her so much.

She went into McDonald's. She usually stopped off there after school for a milk shake with all her friends, and found herself drawn there. It was a safe destination. She changed out of her school clothes, which she stuffed behind the cistern in the Ladies loo. She had a little money, thirty pounds, which her godmother had sent with her birthday card.

Jasmine didn't have a plan, she just knew she couldn't go back home or back to school, not for now anyway. It was still early and Jasmine drifted in and out of the shops in the big, new shopping centre. Eventually she got bored and made her way to the tube station, where she bought a single ticket to Oxford Circus. She had always wanted to go there with her friends to see the shops.

As she emerged from the station, she was swept along in the mass of people who bustled along the pavement. Tourists mingled with shoppers and people criss-crossed the road in front of the red buses and taxis. For a minute or two Jasmine felt a sense of panic welling up inside her. She was used to the more sedate surroundings of her local shopping centre, and this was a real shock. She had to dodge into a store to escape the heaving crowd and catch her breath.

Jasmine felt for her phone. She was going to text Michaela and tell her everything was all right. But she suddenly realised it was no longer in her jacket pocket, and neither was her purse. Frantically Jasmine felt in all her pockets but there was no sign of them. She had been pick-pocketed! She hadn't had a plan when she'd left school, she'd just intended to teach everyone a lesson and get them to understand how she felt about the decision her parents had taken. But now she was starting to get scared. She had no money and no phone.

❖ ❖ ❖

After taking the register, Miss Vine told the class to read a chapter of the book they were studying. Then she hurried to see the Headmaster.

John Turnbull was a jovial character who prided himself on knowing every pupil at his school, not only by name but by sight.

He was helped by the rows and rows of passport-type photos with names underneath, that covered one wall of his office.

'Miss Vine would like to have a word, Headmaster,' said Mrs Burton, his secretary, in her efficient way.

'Ah, come in, Diana,' came his voice. 'What can I do for you?'

'I think we've got a problem with Jasmine Braithwaite. She walked out of school this morning and I'm worried about her.'

'Jasmine Braithwaite,' said Mr Turnbull, jumping up and looking at his wall of photos. "Ah, Jasmine Braithwaite, number 88. That's interesting. I got an email from her mother yesterday, asking for a meeting.'

'It's certainly out of character,' said Miss Vine. 'Jasmine is such a bright, well-balanced and popular girl.'

'I'll get Mrs Burton to give her mother a call.'

The bank had been busy that morning and Jasmine's mother had been flat-out. Tom, the manager, popped his head round the door and made a phone sign with his hand. 'Marcia, your daughter's school is on the phone. You can take it in my office.'

'Oh, it's probably about my meeting with the Head,' said Marcia, hurrying into his small office. 'Hello, Marcia Braithwaite here.'

'Hello, this is Mrs Burton, from Jibson School. Now, there's nothing to worry about, but we were just wondering if there is any reason Jasmine might leave school this morning. Is she with you?'

'What do you mean, leave school? She went in as normal, I saw her get on the tram. I'm at work. She isn't with me....Where is she?'

'Now don't get alarmed, Mrs Braithwaite, I sure there's a perfectly good explanation. It appears that she was upset. She had an argument with one of the other girls and stormed off. She's probably gone home. Can you check and call me back?'

Marcia's heart was racing. Her finger slammed the buttons on the phone. There was a slight pause, and the metallic voice came back. 'The mobile phone you have called is switched off, please try later.'

Next she punched in the number of the home

phone, but the answering machine kicked in after two rings.

'Everything all right?' Tom was standing at the door, looking concerned.

'No, Tom. Jasmine's walked out of school and her phone's not answering!'

'You'd better go off.... Give me a call and let me know what's happening.'

Dave's white van roared along Cromer Road and slid to a halt outside number 73, just as Marcia was putting her key in the door. The burglar alarm beeped loudly, making Marcia's heart sink. It would have been switched off if Jasmine was at home.

Dave ran up the path and went through the same thought process. 'Where the hell is she, Marcia?' he yelled, as he stabbed in the code to turn off the alarm.

'Let's phone the police...' said Marcia, her voice trembling.

Dave was already on his mobile. 'Police, please.'

❖ ❖ ❖

Jasmine was beginning to get hungry. She caught the smell of burgers as she walked past dozens of fast-food outlets on the crowded street.

The crowd all seemed to be going in the opposite direction from her, and she was jostled and pushed again and again as she walked aimlessly along. Finally she reached the end of Oxford Street, where the shops were less crowded, and the towering Centerpoint cast a dark shadow along Charing Cross Road.

Before she reached the junction with Tottenham Court Road, Jasmine turned right into a side street and headed past a couple of sleazy sex shops towards the glimmering neon signs of Soho. The surroundings changed and the bright shops and stores gave way to numerous restaurants, bars and cafes.

Like most of her friends, Jasmine didn't wear a watch, so without her phone she had no idea what time it was. But she knew it must be getting late, as the corner pubs were filling with workers gathering for their evening drinks. They spilled out on to the pavements, forcing her to step out on to the narrow street. People were laughing loudly, greeting each other with double kisses and hugs.

She wondered what it was like to be older, to have a job and be independent. Everyone seemed so happy, so full of excitement. She gazed into the windows of restaurants and saw people studying menus. They looked happy too but they were oblivious to her. It was as if she was invisible.

Gradually the sky between the high buildings was turning dark blue and a chill began to overwhelm the weakening sunlight.

More and more people began to crowd into the narrow streets. Many headed for the big theatre on the corner, others packed themselves into the already crowded pubs and bars.

Jasmine had never been to this part of London before. Her senses were almost overpowered by the myriad sights and sounds. The smells and the lights were intoxicating but she couldn't help noticing the seedier side of things too: dark alleys and doorways with brightly lit stairways leading up to blank doors; sex shops and strip clubs with doormen standing outside, wearing black leather jackets and gold earrings. They eyed the groups of youths who stood gawping at the pictures of undressed women surrounding the entrance.

'Hello, young lady,' said a man's voice. 'You look lost.'

Jasmine glanced up into the face of a man aged about forty. He was dressed in jeans and a green fleece jacket. His smile revealed yellow teeth and his chin was covered in grey stubble.

'I'm not lost, I know where I am, thanks,' retorted Jasmine.

'Oh, I see, it's just that you seem a bit out of it... where's your mum?'

'She's not with me. I'm meeting her later....' Jasmine tried to walk faster, but there were too many people on the pavements and she kept having to stop every few yards.

The man was walking casually alongside her now. 'My name's Jim. I work in the theatre over there, backstage. I'm just on my break. What's your name?'

For some inexplicable reason Jasmine blurted out, 'Katie.'

'Well, Katie, you want to be careful round here. A lot of bad people.' He nodded towards the leather jackets. 'Look, why don't I buy you a hotdog and a Coke. I've only got a fifteen-minute break, then you can go and meet your mother. I don't feel right just leaving you round here. You'll be safe with me.' He grinned again reassuringly.

The thought of a hotdog and a Coke made Jasmine's mouth water. She glanced over at the leather jackets. Two of them were looking her way like hungry dogs.

Jim shared a joke with the foreign-sounding man who sold him the two warm hotdogs from the wheeled container. He handed her one and sat down on a wall, patting the space next to him. The onions and ketchup squirted out of the ends as she bit hungrily into it.

Jim laughed. 'You're a messy one, aren't you?'

Jasmine didn't care though. She was so hungry, it was gone in a few seconds. She washed it down with the warm Coke and wiped her mouth with the back of her hand.

Jim watched her as he finished his. 'You on the run?' he said suddenly.

'Not exactly... I just needed to get away. My parents are being horrible to me.'

'Ah, parents... yeah, who needs them? Where are you staying tonight, Katie?'

It hadn't occurred to Jasmine that she was going to need somewhere to sleep. She had just thought she would keep walking around until she felt her parents had suffered enough. But suddenly her situation hit her like a bombshell. Here she was in the middle of London, on her own with no money and no phone. It was cold and it was getting very late.

'I must get going.' She stood up and began to walk

away.

'Hey, Katie, not so fast. I told you this is a dangerous place and I just bought you a hotdog. The least you can do is sit here until my break's over.'

'Can I borrow your phone?'

'Battery's gone,' shrugged Jim, looking at his phone. 'There's a phone box round the corner.'

The walls of the red phone box were covered in cards showing naked girls with their phone numbers. The floor was wet and it smelled disgusting.

Jasmine lifted the receiver but the wire was ripped clean out of it. She glanced through the dirty window and saw Jim leaning against the wall, laughing and chatting to a black man with long dreadlocks. They clasped hands and gave a high five and he walked off.

Jim came over. 'Bloody vandals,' he said, looking at the damaged phone. 'Never mind, there's another one round the corner....'

❖ ❖ ❖

Outside 73 Cromer Road, a police car was parked, its blue light flashing.

Inside, Marcia sat hunched on the front-room sofa,

57

her face streaked with tears. Next to her sat a female PC, holding a box of tissues in one hand, resting the other on her shoulder. Dave was on his feet, pacing nervously up and down. 'Where the hell is she? It's been hours now.'

A police officer came down the stairs carrying Jasmine's computer and her diary. 'We need to look at these. They may give us a clue as to where she's gone. We'd like you both to come down to the station to have a look at some CCTV footage we've located.'

Marcia was familiar with the police station. As chair of the local Neighborhood Watch group she was often there to speak to the Chief Superintendent, Damien Strong, about various issues such as drug pushers and prostitutes in the local area.

When she and Dave arrived, he was waiting with a concerned look on his face. 'Marcia, Dave... try not to worry, we're doing everything we can. I've got cars out scouring the streets and we've put out a general alert to all the Met regions. And we've visited all her friends' homes.'

'Your PC said you had some CCTV footage,' interrupted Dave.

'Yes, come this way, there's something else....'

Marcia flinched at the words and looked up at Dave. 'What...what else...what is it?'

They entered a darkened room. Four flickering screens were arranged on a desk, with VCRs underneath them.

Damien nodded to an officer who was seated at the desk. 'This is Detective Sergeant Wright, he's looking after this case.'

The policeman leant forward and pushed a button, and one of the screens flickered into life. 'We picked her up on CCTV at exactly 10.07 this morning in the High Street. There she is, going into McDonald's....'

Marcia and Dave watched, transfixed, as they saw the fuzzy image of their daughter dressed in her school clothes entering the door of McDonald's.

Marcia let out a little moan and started to cry again.

Dave put his hand on her shoulder. 'They're going to find her, love....'

Detective Sergeant Wright pressed fast-forward and then play. 'Six minutes later she came out again. But she wasn't wearing her school clothes any more....'

Marcia and Dave watched the picture in

astonishment, as they saw Jasmine's blurred figure on the screen, this time wearing her jeans and a hoodie....

Damian flicked on the lights and picked up a plastic bag. 'We found these in the toilets, stuffed behind the cistern in McDonalds, and they're hers all right, the name tag's in the blazer.... It looks as if she planned this, Mrs Braithwaite. Can you think of any reason your daughter would want to run away?'

Chapter Six

In Soho the atmosphere on the streets was beginning to change. Rain, almost turning to sleet, was starting to fall heavily, and low rumbles of thunder could be heard high above in the darkening London sky.

Revellers spilled out of the bars and pubs and mingled with crowds of people leaving the early performance at the theatre.

The grins on people's faces were now because of the amount of alcohol they had drunk, and some were staggering and talked loudly as rickshaws flew crazily amongst them, splashing through puddles, sending sheets of water on to the pavements.

Jasmine was following Jim along the seething street. He dived left into a quieter alley, where a girl was being violently sick, watched by her boyfriend who was peeing against an overflowing rubbish bin.

She was getting scared now, but Jim was her only hope. She was unsure where she was and she badly wanted to call her parents. 'I thought you had to go back to work?' she panted.

'Yeah, I got my mate Charlie to cover for me.....
the Rasta guy you saw me talking to. Here's another
phone box. Try calling your folks,' he said, opening
the door for her and peering in.... 'Oh dear, it's broken
too. Come on, it's pouring down, let's get under
cover.'

Jim led her back towards the busy street, where he
turned quickly into a dimly lit coffee bar. Standing in
the doorway was a young girl. Her damp blonde hair
hung limply round her pasty face, from which two pale
blue eyes stared blankly. The nails on her small hands
were broken and grubby, and between two of them
she held a half-finished cigarette. Jim grabbed her arm
and steered her inside towards an empty table. Jasmine
noticed her face seemed to twitch with a mixture of
fear and joy.

'This is my girlfriend, Sheena.' Jim leant forward
and roughly kissed the top of the girl's head. 'This is
Katie... she's run away from her parents so I'm taking
care of her.'

Jasmine was confused. The girl didn't look much
older than she was but she wore lots of make-up, and
her lip was pierced with a silver ring.

'Parents are crap... you're better off without

them,' Sheena said, shrugging her shoulders.

Jim returned with three coffees. 'Sheena and me are best mates, aren't we, sweetheart?'

Sheena nodded, her eyes avoiding his.

'Look, I was thinking, you can shack up with us for the night. In the morning you can figure out what to do next…. Can't she, Sheena?' said Jim, his voice hardening.

'Well, I… I don't know… if…' stammered Jasmine, thinking of her warm bed at home.

'It'll be OK,' smiled Sheena, glancing at Jim. 'You can sleep on the sofa… it'll be an adventure.'

The night bus was crowded. Jasmine tried to wipe the condensation from the window but it just smeared into a watery film and made her hand wet. 'Where are we?' she said, trying to peer into the darkness.

'Camden,' said Sheena, getting to her feet. 'This is our stop.'

Jim herded them both down the stairs and out on to the sodden pavement. His place turned out to be a two-room flat in a large terraced house which smelt damp and musty.

Jim closed the door firmly behind them. 'You'll be fine here,' he said, smiling his wolfish grin.

❖ ❖ ❖

DS Wright stood up and looked at the photo that Jasmine's parents had given him. He picked it up and studied it for a moment. 'Did she give any indication she was going to run off?'

Marcia put down the cup of tea she was sipping, and looked angrily at DS Wright. 'We've told you a dozen times, this is totally out of the blue. It's just not like her to do anything without telling us first. Sure, she was upset last night when we told her we were moving to Barbados, but she never threatened to run off or anything like that.'

'We are fed up with the kind of life she's being exposed to here in Britain,' interrupted Dave. 'That's why we're moving to Barbados. They have more discipline there and kids are taught to have respect.'

'Kids can be so stroppy these days, can't they? I mean, sometimes you just want to give them a good smack, don't you?' The DS laughed, but his eyes stayed focused on Dave.

'If you mean, did we hit her...we have never laid a hand on her.... We don't believe in that sort of thing,' exclaimed Dave.

'Of course, but not everyone does....'

'Are you trying to say we are to blame for her running off?' Marcia looked astonished.

'No one is saying anything,' said DS Wright. 'But we have to establish the full picture. I can imagine she's a bit upset about being dragged off to a strange place and leaving all her friends behind.'

'Barbados is not a strange place and she can make new friends when she gets there,' said Dave defensively.

The DS looked at his watch. 'She's been missing for twelve hours now. If nothing has been heard by ten in the morning we should go public and let the TV and newspapers know. If anybody knows where she is they might come forward. I suggest you go home and get some sleep. If we hear anything I'll call straight away.'

He held the door open for Dave and Marcia before turning to his colleague. 'Not much to go on with this one. There's no record of her chatting to anyone on the net. It doesn't look good.'

❖ ❖ ❖

'I'm going out. I've got a bit of business to do.' Jim glanced at Sheena. 'Look after her and give her a duvet.' He closed the door and Jasmine heard the key turn in the lock.

Sheena seemed to breathe more easily once Jim had gone and she brightened up. 'He's off to do a bit of dealing. That's how he makes his money.'

'I thought he worked at the theatre.'

'Is that what he told you?' She laughed. She offered Jasmine a cigarette and held out the dirty cup she was drinking red wine from.

'No thanks,' said Jasmine. 'I don't smoke or drink.'

Sheena laughed another harsh laugh. 'Drink helps....'

'My parents don't drink much, they say it's not good for you.'

Sheena stared blankly at her. 'Wait a minute, your parents are still together and they don't drink?'

'Well, yes,' said Jasmine, a note of surprise in her voice.

'Why did you run away then?'

'Because I wanted to make them change their minds.'

'About what?'

'Moving to Barbados.'

Sheena stared in disbelief at Jasmine. 'Let me get

this straight....You ran away from home because your parents want to move to Barbados?'

'Yes, I don't want to leave my school and all my friends. It's not fair!'

Sheena burst out laughing. But this time it sounded more like sobbing, and ended in a rasping cough.

'Why did you run away?' asked Jasmine.

Sheena poured the last of the wine into her cup and gulped it down. 'My dad used to beat my mother up every night when he got home. Then she started to drink. It got so bad she was downing two bottles of this a day.' Sheena held up the empty wine bottle. 'She spent the whole day just lying on the sofa. Then, when my dad walked out, my mum found a boyfriend. Uncle George I had to call him. He was a drunk too and after a while he started come into my room late at night and get a bit too friendly... if you know what I mean. So on my fourteenth birthday I decided to leave. I met Jim in Soho. He said he would take care of me.... So here I am.'

Jasmine felt sick. Suddenly her situation hit her with full force. How could she be so stupid, so childish, so spoilt? Compared to Sheena she had a wonderful life. 'Jim said there was a phone I could use.'

Sheena shook her head. 'There's no phone here.

Jim's got a mobile.'

Just then Jasmine heard the key turn in the lock and Jim came in. He looked angry and wet.

'Fix me a drink,' he snapped. 'Bloody cops... nearly got busted and I had to dump my stash. All I'm trying to do is make a living.'

Sheena looked scared as he sat down heavily on the sofa beside her. 'We need to make some dosh fast.' He glanced at Sheena and then his eyes turned to Jasmine. 'Do you like parties, Katie?'

'Yes....'

'Good, well you'd better get some beauty sleep, cos tomorrow we're going to one.'

'Can I use your phone, please?' asked Jasmine.

'Sorry, love, I've run out of credit. I'll top it up tomorrow. Now, you get some sleep.'

❖ ❖ ❖

Marcia and Dave didn't sleep much that night. They kept the television on in the bedroom, tuned to the news. Half hoping nothing would come on about Jasmine and half hoping it would.

'No news is good news,' Dave kept saying.

'Will you stop saying that, it makes no sense!'

snapped Marcia. 'I want to hear any news.... I want to hear that she's safe.'

❖ ❖ ❖

Next morning, Jim, wearing grubby tracksuit bottoms and a stained vest, shuffled out of the filthy kitchen carrying a cup of coffee. He flicked on the television and stood in front of it, scratching his armpit.

'Looks like rain again,' he said, reaching to change the channel. But before he could, a picture of Jasmine appeared on the screen. It showed her going into McDonalds and coming out wearing different clothes. Then it cut to a video of her laughing and happy at home, and a close-up photo of her filled the screen again, as a solemn voice gave a number to call if anyone had any information.

'Oh, brilliant!' shouted Jim at the TV. He turned to Jasmine, who lay cowering on the sofa under the filthy duvet. 'You told me your name was Katie,' he screamed at her. 'Now you're plastered all over the news and it turns out you're called Jasmine and the Fuzz are looking all over the place for you.'

Jasmine jumped up and stood shaking, next to Sheena, who had lit her first cigarette of the day and was staring at the picture of Jasmine's face on the TV.

'We've got to get rid of her,' she coughed through the smoke. 'The cops will say we kidnapped her or something. Give her some money for the bus and let her go.'

'No way,' snarled Jim. 'I've got a bloke who's willing to give me a hundred quid to take her to the party and I need the dosh....You'd better tell her about what's expected when she gets there. I don't want any trouble from her. Now I'm going to get some breakfast at the cafe.' He turned and walked out, closing and double-locking the door.

Jasmine was still shaking. 'Why would someone give a hundred pounds to him to take me to a party? I don't understand.'

'Katie, I mean Jasmine... you're pretty thick, aren't you? It's not going to be a birthday party with balloons and jelly and cake, you idiot.'

Jasmine looked back at her blankly.

'Look, all you have to do is be nice to the men and you'll be fine. Sometimes they slip you twenty quid, but you have to give that to Jim. He calls it rent money.'

'Oh my God!' Jasmine sobbed desperately. 'Oh no! I want to go home... I feel sick... I don't want to go to any party. I don't want to do that sort of thing, I don't want to be 'nice' to men.'

As Sheena looked at her, a strange look came into her eyes, as if she was remembering... seeing her own innocence in Jasmine. She went over to the bedroom and came out with a tatty-looking teddy bear. 'If Jim finds out I did this he'll kill me.' She dug her fingers into a hole in the back of the bear and pulled out a twenty-pound note. 'Here, take this. I've been stashing it, should be enough to get you home in a cab.'

Jasmine stared blankly at the dirty, crumpled note.

'Now you hide behind the door and when he comes back, run for it. I'll keep him occupied.' She walked over to the window and looked out. 'He's coming back now,' she hissed urgently. 'Over here.' She grabbed Jasmine by the shoulders.

Jasmine was standing with her arms hanging limply at her sides, her bottom lip quivering, her eyes staring wildly.

Sheena put her face inches from Jasmine's and spoke commandingly. 'Listen, you'll only get one chance at this. Do as I say. Stand behind the door and when he comes in, run for it, and keep running until you reach the end of the road. Try to get into a taxi as quick as you can. Do you hear me?'

Jasmine nodded, but she couldn't stop shaking.

Sheena pushed Jasmine roughly behind the door and half hid her with a coat that was hanging on a hook. 'Now, wait until he comes through, then get out and run,' she hissed.

Jasmine could hear Jim's heavy steps coming up the stairs. They mingled with the thumping of her heart, which was beating so hard she thought it would burst through her chest.

As the key turned in the lock and the door slowly opened, Sheena's voice came urgently from the bathroom. 'Quick, Jim, in here. I think she's dying!'

'What the hell?' Jim rushed across the room towards the bathroom, leaving the door swinging open behind him.

Jasmine lurched from behind it and almost fell over as she fled headlong down the stairs. Before she reached the front door she could hear Jim's voice yelling.

A sharp crack, followed by a piercing scream, was the last thing she heard as she burst into the daylight, almost falling down the six steps on to the pavement.

She could see the busy road just ahead, with buses

and cars moving noisily along it. Her legs almost turned to jelly but fear pumped adrenaline into her muscles and she ran like she had never run before.

Only when she reached the corner did she look back. Jim was standing at the doorway, his right fist clenched above his head, his left hand holding Sheena by her lank blonde hair. Her face was twisted in pain and blood had splattered from her nose on to her white T-shirt.

A taxi was coming along the road and Jasmine flung herself in front of it, waving her arms wildly. The cabbie jammed on the brakes and leant out of his window. 'Hey, take it easy, love, I nearly had you then.'

Jasmine thrust the screwed-up twenty pound note at him. '73 Cromer Road... please,' she panted wildly.

'All right, sweetheart, take it easy... jump in.'

As the cab drove along, the driver kept looking suspiciously in his mirror at Jasmine. Then he suddenly hit the steering wheel. 'That's it, now I remember... you're the young girl on the telly who's gone missing!' He reached for his radio, and within minutes a police car sped up alongside the cab and pulled up sharply in front of it.

Jasmine was bundled into the back seat next to

a woman PC who kept smiling and asking her if everything was all right. Jasmine was in a daze, she couldn't speak. All she wanted to do was get home.

It seemed to take ages to get things sorted out. First Jasmine was examined by the police doctor and was asked loads of questions about what had happened. She wasn't allowed to go straight home, but was interviewed by Social Services who wanted to know why she had run off and asked how her parents treated her.

Jasmine's biggest concern was for Sheena, who had so bravely saved her and had suffered because of it. 'Please, you must help her,' she pleaded with the police. She gave them a description of Jim and, as best she could, described where the house was.

Next day DS Wright told her Jim had been arrested and charged with drug dealing, assault and child prostitution.

'But where is Sheena?' asked Jasmine

'I'll find out,' promised DS Wright. 'Social Services will have taken over, but we'll try to find out what's happened to her.'

When she was finally allowed to see her parents she realised how much they meant to her, and the tearful reunion lasted at least half an hour before they made their way home from the police station.

❖ ❖ ❖

It was a week before Jasmine returned to school, where she was met with a mixture of odd looks and celebrity status.

Michaela, Rachel and Sam stayed close to her all day and warded off the stupid comments and questions from Germaine Dobson and her cronies.

But mostly people just stared at her, unsure of what to say....

After a while things started to get back to normal. At home the atmosphere was still tense and the subject was avoided, especially at mealtimes, when Mum would keep staring at her and giving little, forced smiles whenever she looked at her.

Her dad, however, was different. The episode had made him even more determined to go through with the move.

It was hard for him to disguise his anger at what Jasmine had done. His Caribbean background made him feel ashamed that his daughter had run away and brought shame on the family. 'This is exactly why we're going,' he said firmly. 'In Barbados everyone knows each other. It's safer.'

'Don't kid yourself, Dave,' Marcia said. 'There are bad people everywhere and Barbados has its fair share of problems.'

'I know,' agreed Dave. 'It's just on a smaller scale, and the quality of life is so much better, and people look out for one another, not like here where you don't even know who your neighbours are. This running away thing has made my mind up. We're going, and that's final.'

Jasmine realised that she had to accept the decision and this continued to make her very depressed. The only positive thing that had come out of the episode was that Sheena was now safe.

DC Wright had made some enquiries, and it turned out that Social Services had put Sheena in touch with Barnardo's and she was doing really well at one of their projects.

Jim had been taken to court and had ended up in prison. Just the thought of him always made Jasmine shiver. 'What if…?'

The following months sped past. The house sold more quickly than expected and Dad went off to Barbados. When he left, Jasmine couldn't help hating him for going through with the move. She had secretly hoped he would change his mind. But at least she still had some time to be with her friends, and Mum seemed a bit more sympathetic about allowing her out.

Jasmine wanted to stop the world and pause time, but before she knew it, Michaela, Rachel and Sam were organising a leaving party at the local pizza restaurant. They wanted to give Jasmine a good send-off.

It was the end of term and everyone was looking forward to the summer holidays and moving up a year when they got back to school. But Jasmine's departure had cast a shadow over her friends' celebrations. They had been best pals since they had started school, and although they tried hard to make jokes and laugh there was an air of sadness around the table.

'I've bought you a present,' said Michaela, handing Jasmine a T-shirt with "Friends for Eternity"on the front.

'So have I,' said Sam, holding up a tiny teddy-bear with a red bow round its neck.

'Me too!' said Rachel. 'It's a charm bracelet. It's only got one charm,' she continued apologetically, 'but you can add more whenever you like.'

It was the moment Jasmine had been dreading

and the tears flowed freely as she hugged Michaela, Rachel and Sam in turn. It was hurting so much to leave them. She promised to text each of them every day and to chat online as usual. They of course all promised to come and visit as soon as they could. But deep in her heart she felt as if her world was ending and she was acting in some kind of play.

❖ ❖ ❖

As the cab turned off the motorway towards the airport Jasmine felt as if the last year had been the most tumultuous of her short life, and now she was being sucked in to a vortex from which there was no escape. Beyond it lay the unknown.

Chapter Seven

The afternoon heat hit Jasmine in the face and penetrated deep into her chest as she stepped out of the plane at Grantley Adams Airport, Barbados. It was a heat such as she had never felt before, and, mingled with the strong smell of aviation fuel, it made a nauseating cocktail.

Unlike the airport in London, passengers walked across the shimmering tarmac from the plane to the terminal building, which had been designed to look like a group of futuristic white tents. Even though it was only a short distance, Jasmine's face was beaded with perspiration before she got into the air-conditioned building where suitcases were already dropping on to the carousel.

It was not long before they were wheeling their luggage through the arrivals lounge and out once more into the sweltering heat.

Dad was waiting anxiously at the exit.

Jasmine saw him first and instinctively ran into his

open arms. 'Dad, you look great,' she said, stepping back to get a good look.

Even though it had only been six months, he looked different. His face was darker and the sun had made him look healthier. His clothes were different too. Gone were his usual jeans and fleece jacket. He now wore a white T-shirt and a pair of khaki shorts.

He seemed to fit right in with the groups of minibus and taxi drivers who thronged around the airport exit, many holding signs with passenger names on them.

'Well, the island life suits me,' he laughed.

Mum soon caught up with them, accompanied by a red-hatted porter, his trolley creaking under the weight of the two large suitcases which contained the last of the clothes and personal items they had packed.

Mum threw her arms around her husband lovingly. 'Great to see you again. We've missed you.'

'Me too,' he said as he gave her another kiss.

Jasmine rolled her eyes in embarrassment.

'Let me go get the truck,' said Dad, breaking away from Marcia.

While he brought the pick-up truck round from the car park, Jasmine stood in the shade and watched as the wealthy tourists who had travelled first class were met by limousines, which would take them to the expensive hotels that stretched along the west coast of the island.

Barbados was a place where many very rich people had homes and came to holiday. The island had been known as Little Britain, complete with its own Nelson's Column and at one time Trafalgar Square. But the Bajans didn't like that legacy any more. They wanted their own identity.

However, tourism was the main source of income for Barbados, and there were hundreds of spectacular developments being built all over the island, villas surrounded by golf courses, apartment blocks and houses with their own moorings for luxury yachts.

This meant there was going to be lots of work for her dad. It had been the centre of all the discussions, when her parents had been making their decision to move to Barbados. Dad's kitchen and bathroom building firm was doing fine in London, but there would be even more work in Barbados, and well-paid work too.

Already he had been contracted to fit kitchens and bathrooms in a new development and he was due to start work in a couple of weeks' time.

They left the airport and headed along the Tom Adams Highway towards Bridgetown. Jasmine was pleasantly surprised by the beautiful houses she saw and hoped theirs was going to be the same. Their new home was situated in the Parish of St. James, right on the West Coast.

❖ ❖ ❖

Summerland House, and the land it was on, had been in her dad's family for generations, but it had lain empty for ten years or more. Now it was worth a lot of money due to its proximity to the expensive hotels and apartments near the Sandy Lane mega-luxury hotel and golf course. Originally it had been built by Grannie Braithwaite's Great-Grandfather Leonard and his wife Mathilda, and it had been passed down over the decades.

Great-Great-Grandfather Leonard was the son of a freed slave called Prince Henry, a ship builder and seafaring man who, after the abolition of slavery, had made a small fortune transporting goods from island to island in his fleet of small schooners.

When Leonard died, Mathilda had stayed in the house, until she passed away, aged 100.

There had been a lot of arguing about what to do with it, between her children and grandchildren. So much so that the house and the land had become even more derelict. The garden was a mass of overgrown bushes and thick vines that had crept everywhere, almost covering the house.

Each time one of the family had came up with a plan to do something with the land the others disagreed, and so nothing was done.

Eventually, one by one they had passed away, until only Grannie Braithwaite, the youngest, survived. And she became the sole owner.

She had let her son, Dave, Jasmine's dad, rebuild the house and live there, as he was going to inherit the land anyway when she died.

It had taken Dave months to put the place back to its former glory. He was proud of his work, and was anxious to show it off. 'There you are, Jazzie,' he said, turning off the main road. 'Your new home.'

Jasmine looked up at the house facing towards the coast. Surprisingly, it was better than she had expected – but she didn't let on.

The house was built from the local creamy-pink coral stone with a bright blue, tiled roof. It was all on one floor and a driveway led up to the front door through a large garden, which was mostly coarse grass edged by a low wall made from the same coral stone.

There were a number of mature bushes and trees which had been cut back and were now looking healthy and verdant. Here and there were aloe plants, their long, cactus-like spiky leaves pointing upwards like green flames.

Jasmine got out of the truck and walked up the stairs to find a large, open veranda with tables and chairs spread out like a living room. Despite herself she felt a tinge of excitement looking out over the garden and seeing the blue Caribbean sea beyond. Her footsteps echoed along the wooden floors as she inspected the big, airy rooms with their shuttered windows.

'Well, what do you think, girls?' asked Dad nervously.

'It's beautiful, Dave,' said Mum. 'I love what you've done with it. I can't wait to do the finishing touches.'

'You know I always leave that sort of thing to you.'

Jasmine was staring out of the window, trying not to look interested.

'Well Jazzie, what do you think?' Dad said anxiously.

Jasmine shrugged. 'It's all right,' she said flatly.

Dave looked hurt.

'She's tired, Dave, the time difference is starting to tell on her,' said her mum. 'Why don't you get some sleep, darlin', you'll feel better in the morning,' she said to Jasmine, putting her arm round her.

Jasmine's room was spacious, with a large window all the way along one side. A large, bladed fan in the middle of the ceiling spun slowly round, stirring the icy breeze that came from the air-conditioning unit on the wall above her bed.

Well, this is it, she thought to herself as she lay in the darkness, listening to the muted hum of the air-conditioning and the incessant chirping of the frogs and crickets outside.

Through the window opposite her bed she could see the deep velvet-blue night sky, studded with thousands of stars. The huge moon floated over the Caribbean sea like a giant yellow orb, its reflection shimmering in a straight silver path. It stretched towards her across the waves, from the horizon to the pale, sandy beach.

Jasmine thought of her room back in Cromer

Road. You couldn't see very much from the window there at night. Just the grey brick walls of the terraced houses opposite and the orange glare of the street light outside.

Well, at least the surroundings are nice, she thought, as her eyes closed and she fell into a deep, restful sleep.

Chapter Eight

Next morning, the rising sun blasted through the window, eliminating any chance of further sleep. It was so bright it hurt Jasmine's eyes and she fumbled for her sunglasses.

For a minute or two she was disorientated. She lay there, looking round the room, trying to remember the layout of the house. She heard voices coming from the other side of her door and recognised her mother's laugh.

She sounds happy enough, thought Jasmine, as she pulled on a pair of shorts and a T-shirt. She absent-mindedly scratched a large bump that had mysteriously appeared on her arm – it itched like crazy.

It was odd not going downstairs to breakfast, and it was even odder to find Mum and Dad sitting on the veranda at the breakfast table under a canvas awning. Small, colourful birds fluttered amongst the bushes, and a couple of bright yellow butterflies cavorted backwards and forwards, as if they were celebrating the dawning of a new day.

'Sleep well, Jazzie?' her mother greeted her with a smile.

'Yeah, but I've got this really itchy bump on my arm,' replied Jasmine.

'Oh, it's a mosquito bite, I've got some cream for them,' said Mum.

Jasmine didn't realise that mosquito bites were something she was going to have to get used to.

Dad got up from the table and stretched his arms above his head.

'No time for sitting around here. I've got to get over to see Mr O'Brien about the final contract to put in the kitchens and bathrooms for the development.'

'Oh, can you drop us at your mum's first? Me and Jazzie can't wait to say hello.'

'Sure,' said Dave, 'and you can ask her about the arrangement for looking after Jasmine, as well.'

'Yes, it will be a great help if she can do it... and don't worry about picking us up. We'll get the bus back.'

❖ ❖ ❖

Grannie Braithwaite lived alone in a small house in

Bathsheba, a beautiful town on the rugged, windswept Atlantic coast of the island.

Dad dropped Jasmine and her mother at the top of the steep hill which led down towards the craggy beach with its huge, towering rocks sticking out of the foaming sea. Grannie Braithwaite's house was a small, pretty, wooden building, perched precariously on the hillside above the beach.

Its pink fence was interlaced with flowering plants and the small garden overflowed with beautiful shrubs and trees. At the front of the house was a wide balcony with a large, brightly coloured three-seater swinging chair. In front of this was a low table, on which sat a vase of flowers and a jug and tall, striped, multicoloured glasses.

At the other end of the balcony was a narrow, wicker dining table surrounded by four matching chairs. A creaking overhead fan was fixed to the wooden ceiling and it rotated lazily, stirring the warm air without any real effect.

Rusty nails and hinges, attacked by the ferocious salty air, dribbled orange trails down the white walls and window frames.

Jasmine and her mum's arrival was announced by the sharp yapping of a small brown dog who came rushing towards them, only to decide the effort was too much. It promptly lay down in the shade under the six wooden steps which led up from the path to the porch.

'Pay no mind to him,' chuckled Grannie Braithwaite, leaning on the doorway. 'He likes the sound of his own bark.'

Grannie Braithwaite was a sprightly seventy-year-old, with a full head of pure white hair. Her dark brown skin, although creased with age, shone with a healthy vitality.

She stood at the top of the steps with her arms outstretched, her eyes twinkling with a benevolent, energetic and somehow knowing look, which seemed to envelop Jasmine with the warmth of her soul.

Jasmine had only met her once and that was on her first visit to Barbados when she was only two years old. She couldn't remember it. But now, for some reason, she felt overjoyed to be seeing her grandmother again. It was as if they had a spiritual link.

'Grannie B!' she cried, leaping up the stairs into the waiting arms which clamped around her with overwhelming love.

After the hug, which seemed to go on for minutes,

Grannie Braithwaite turned to Jasmine's mum. 'Marcia, look at you now. You look the happiest I've seen.... How you settlin' in?'

'Fine! Dave's done a great job on the house and I can't wait to finish it off. I've got an interview with the bank at Sunset Crest in two weeks, so that will give me some time to get everything sorted out.'

'I must come and see what David has done with the old house. Y'know it's been years since I saw it.' Grannie Braithwaite shook her head. 'It's always been a source of upset to me, so much squabbling. And for what?'

'You'll love it now,' said Mum proudly. 'Yes, you must come over soon.'

'And what about you, Jasmine? How are you settling in?'

'Oh I've only been here a day, Grannie B... and look, I got bitten by a mosquito.'

'The best thing for that is aloe vera. I'll cut a piece from the garden.'

Grannie Braithwaite took a sharp knife and sliced off a piece of the spiky plant and rubbed the milky sap on the bite. It was cool and soothing, and the itching quickly began to ease. By lunchtime, to Jasmine's relief, the itching had all but gone.

She helped Mum to lay the table while Grannie Braithwaite busied herself in her tiny kitchen, and very soon the tantalising smell of macaroni pie and fried flying fish with rice and baked breadfruit was wafting out of the open window.

The food tasted delicious. Jasmine ate until she was so full she had to lie down on the swinging seat and rest.

She looked out towards the sea and listened to the Atlantic waves crashing relentlessly on the rocks. A few intrepid surfers were paddling determinedly out to catch the waves, but this was not a place for inexperienced swimmers.

For this reason the beach was relatively free from tourists, who tended to stick to the calmer, Caribbean side of the island. The constant wind had caused the trees to grow at a crazy angle, branches almost touching the ground as they leant inland, away from the sea and the furious, salty spray.

The landscape above the beach was covered with tough grass, which was kept short by the many black-bellied sheep that roamed the low, scrubby hills above the shoreline. Further back, the land rose higher and the tough shrubs gave way to more luxuriant trees and plants, with the occasional plantation of banana trees, in neat rows, with their clusters of hanging green fruit and purple flowers drooping below.

The steep, winding roads which led away from the coast were dotted with houses similar to Grannie Braithwaite's. Some of them were built from timber, others from concrete breeze-blocks with corrugated iron roofs, thick with red rust. Anything metal was doomed to attack and many old cars which had been left unused outside houses were now rusty hulks. Nothing was impervious to the salt which, like an alien substance from a science fiction film, slowly destroyed everything in its path.

It must have been the jetlag, because slowly Jasmine's eyes closed. The gentle rocking of the chair and the crashing waves lulled her into a luxurious sleep.

She didn't know how long she had slept, but she was awakened by Grannie Braithwaite gently stroking her cheek.

'Time to go, darlin',' she whispered. 'You will come and see me again soon, won't you?'

Jasmine smiled up at her. 'Yes, Grannie B, I will,' she murmered sleepily.

Marcia was pleased that Jasmine had taken to Grannie Braithwaite.'Dave and I were rather hoping you would look after Jasmine and that she could come here after school. If she can do her homework and have something to eat, Dave can pick her up after work, if that's all right? Just while we get ourselves sorted.'

'Of course she can,' said Grannie Braithwaite. 'It will give me a really good chance to get to know my grand-daughter better.'

'Oh, that's great,' said Marcia with relief. 'It will be a real help.'

It was the first Jasmine had heard of this arrangement. Yet another decision made without consulting her. She wondered how she was supposed to get to Grannie Braithwaite's after school every day.

Grannie Braithwaite seemed to sense what she was thinking. 'Don't worry, darlin', there's a bus which will drop you right on the road down there. It's only a twenty-minute ride from your school.'

Grannie Braithwaite's reassurance didn't make her feel much better about the situation. School back in London had been a five-minute tram ride away, and that was via the shopping centre with her friends.

She had only been in Barbados for a day and already she felt that her parents were behaving exactly the same way towards her, not asking her opinion. She just wanted to scream, 'Take me back to London.' She started feeling resentful all over again.

Jasmine didn't say much to her mother on the journey back home.

The bright yellow-and-blue bus, its engine bellowing, careered along the narrow roads towards Bridgetown. Every so often the driver would sound his horn to alert prospective passengers of his approach. When one of them held out their arm the driver would brake in a cloud of dust to pick them up.

Loud music played as the conductor collected the standard fare of two Bajan dollars, and the bus roared on its way, sometimes crazily overtaking another bus.

Jasmine and her mother clung on for dear life as the bus took corners at racing speeds. The rest of the passengers seemed unperturbed by this, and every now and then one would ring the bell and the bus would screech to a halt, allowing them to jump off.

Other passengers eyed Jasmine and her mother curiously. They could see they were definitely not locals - they didn't look at ease as the bus bounced along. Jasmine couldn't put her finger on it. She didn't feel threatened in any way, just slightly uncomfortable, as if she and her mother were intruding on the everyday routine of the passengers.

Her mother felt it too, and tried to make eye contact with a few of the passengers - but to no avail. They just gazed silently ahead, as if deep in thought.

The bus terminated at the busy bus station in the bustling capital of Barbados, Bridgetown, where they would need to change for another to take them up the West Coast road to Prospect Bay.

It was late afternoon and Mum decided to take a look round town before going home. So they walked across the famous bridge which gave the town its name and turned left towards the main street, passing the statue of Lord Nelson, the Government buildings and the church.

The town was thronging with tourists, mainly from the huge cruise ship that was moored in the docks behind the town. There were several large shops selling expensive watches and jewellery, and the big department store, Caves, which stocked everything from designer clothes to washing machines. But the streets behind were full of local people doing their weekend shopping at the market stalls.

Cars drove too quickly along the main road,

blaring out thumping music, and taxi drivers, sitting on a low wall in the shade next to their cabs, called out to tourists, 'Taxi...taxi sir.....'

Jasmine and her mother found their way to the bus stop and within a minute were once again grimly hanging on as the bus driver, steering with one hand while the other pushed the last morsels of a roti into his mouth, exited Bridgetown as if he were being chased by the police.

Quickly the sea appeared on the left, and the bus tore along Spring Garden Highway. Preparations for Crop Over, the huge Carnival held in Barbados, were getting underway and all along the beachfront enrmous tents were being erected and stages built for bands to play on.

Stacks of speakers were being put up to pump out the deafening music, and rum counters were getting ready to cater for the thousands of Carnival-goers who would line the route of the Carnival parade. As the bus sped along Jasmine saw young people about her age gathered in groups along Brighton beach.

'Missing your friends?' said Mum, noticing Jasmine's longing look.

'Yes,' answered Jasmine sulkily. 'But there's nothing I can do about that, is there?'

Chapter Nine

The next day was Saturday and Jasmine was up early. As usual the sun was belting down and the heat was beginning to build up.

After breakfast Dad said they were going down to the West Coast Mall shopping centre in Holetown, which was about five minutes drive away. All Jasmine felt like doing was lying down in her room with the air-con going, but Dad insisted she join them.

West Coast Mall was an up-market shopping precinct situated in Holetown, opposite the beach on the main West Coast road. It was where many of the wealthy residents of the villas, hotels and apartments did their shopping. Dad parked his pick-up truck amongst the SUVs, and he and Mum set off purposefully towards the main supermarket.

'I'll just walk down to the beach for a bit,' said Jasmine.

Shopping with her parents could be a soul-destroying experience at the best of times, but with the new house, Mum had a long list of utensils and household items she wanted to buy. Jasmine knew this was going to be a marathon.

'We'll meet you there when we've finished,' said Mum, pushing the trolley eagerly.

'Yes, I think it's going to be a while - so enjoy!' waved Dad.

They had no worries about Jasmine going off on her own here, unlike the anxieties they would have felt back in London.

The two-lane road was teeming with cars, all travelling extremely fast. Every now and then a couple of buses would roar past, their horns blaring. It was several minutes before there was a safe enough pause for Jasmine to run across to the narrow pavement on the other side. There was a small gap between a restaurant and the high wall of a villa, and a path sloped down about twenty yards before opening on to the soft, white, sandy beach.

Surprisingly, there were few sunbathers on this beach. They were further up, closer to the big hotels. Dad had explained that all the beaches in Barbados were public. No one was allowed to own a private beach so anyone was allowed to use them, although the wealthy tourists tended to congregate near the big hotels, leaving other stretches of beach relatively quiet.

The section Jasmine was standing on was backed by a beach bar, full of wealthy-looking twenty-year-olds, and by the high fence of one of the multi-million dollar houses that were dotted along the coast. 'Keep Out', read the signs on the metal gate which allowed the owners on to the beach.

Jasmine slipped off her flip-flops and curled her toes into the powdery white sand. It felt warm and soft.

She slowly walked down to the water's edge and stood with her feet in the warm water, feeling the crystal clear waves lapping at her legs with a steady slow rhythm, just as they had been doing for centuries, she thought, before men even set foot here.

Her thoughts were interrupted by a burst of laughter accompanied by loud music. It had a frantic beat and the singer rattled out the words of the current Crop Over hit. She remembered hearing the same tune being played in the cars in Bridgetown the day before. It seemed to be everywhere.

The singer, backed by a thumping, infectious, relentless beat, repeatedly chanted, 'English Girl, English Girl, Why y'wanna go home?' The words stayed in her head, tormenting her with the question which she so wanted to scream the answer to.

This time the music was coming from a portable stereo. It was surrounded by a group of five youngsters, who were walking slowly along the beach towards her.

The boy carrying the stereo looked about thirteen. His hair was in braids and his open shirt revealed his skinny brown torso and a thick gold chain. A pair of long shorts clung precariously to his narrow hips and his underpants showed above them. He wore a pair of new-looking trainers, their whiteness gleaming in the sun.

His cocky, over-confident swagger signalled he was trying to look as though he was the leader of the group. But Jasmine noticed he kept looking over his shoulder at the two girls with him, who sat down on the sand, giggling, as he danced to the music. Both of them were about Jasmine's age.

The two other boys watched.... One of them glanced over in Jasmine's direction, his white teeth flashing a smile at her. For a second Jasmine returned the smile instinctively, before her eyes dropped in shocked embarrassment.

She walked a few paces up the beach and sat down

with her back to them, trying to gaze purposefully out to sea. A second or two later she sensed a shadow fall across her back.

'Hey, English girl, you all by yourself?' came the sound of a boy's voice in a heavy Bajan accent, which sounded a bit like a West country English accent.

Jasmine turned and looked up, but her eyes struggled to adjust to the dazzling sun, making her squint blindly up at the speaker.

The boy sat down beside her, and through her watering eyes she saw his face.

'No... my parents are shopping,' she stammered. Then with puzzlement, 'How do you know I'm from England?'

'It's obvious. You just... look English,' he laughed.

Jasmine looked down at her clothes. There was nothing English about them. She wore a simple white T-shirt, a pair of navy-blue shorts and an old pair of flip-flops. It was hardly as if she had a Union Jack painted on her face.

'So, you on vacation?' the boy said, picking up a handful of sand and letting it run through his fingers.

'No, I live here now....'

'Hey, Breezy, aren't you going to introduce us to

your new English geeelfriend?' came another Bajan voice. The other boy, who was also wearing a gold chain, was standing with his hands on his hips. He looked over his shoulder at the two girls, who were still giggling uncontrollably.

'Yeah, I'm Alvin Breeze... but everyone calls me Breezy.'

'Jasmine, Jasmine Braithwaite... but everyone calls me Jazzie.'

'And this is Broderick. Why don't you come over, Jazzie?' he said, getting up and nodding in the direction of the others.

Jasmine got to her feet and followed Breezy and Broderick over to where the girls sat watching her with a mixture of curiosity and contempt. It was obvious they didn't like her from the way they looked at her.

'That's Maxine,' said Breezy, pointing at a tall, gangly girl wearing a bikini top and skin-tight cycling shorts.

The girl just stared at Jasmine, her eyes flicking up and down as if she were assessing the threat she posed. 'And that's Josie.'

A chubby girl looked up and gave a quick grimace, then continued to pat the sand into a small mound before the next wave came and washed it away.

'Hi,' said Jasmine shyly, 'I've just moved here with my mum and dad from the UK. It's beautiful here, isn't it?'

'Your folks rich then, are they?' asked Maxine, still eying her suspiciously.

'Er no... not by these standards,' said Jasmine, turning towards the villa behind her.

'It's owned by foreigners like you,' spat Maxine. 'Tink dey own de place.'

'I'm not a foreigner, my Dad's a Bajan...'

'Yeah, but he only come here now, and where y'mother from?'

'She was born in England but her mother was from Jamaica,' said Jasmine proudly.

The girl sucked her teeth. 'Well, what's she doing here then? Jamaicans always call Barbados a small island.'

Jasmine felt the same confusion she had felt when she was confronted at school in London about her colour for the first time. 'It's time I was going,' she said angrily, putting on her flip-flops.

'What school you goin' to?' said Breezy.

'Whittington,' Jasmine muttered, not really thinking it was any of their business.

'Eh eh... see you there, English Girl, that's where we go too,' shouted Maxine ominously.

'Yeah, see you...' mumbled Jasmine, as she tried to make a dignified exit without falling over on the soft, uneven sand.

That night she lay in bed staring out of her window at the silver strip of sea, still lit by the now-waning moon. She felt lonelier than she had ever felt before in her life.

She couldn't even phone Miki or anyone back home as her mobile was now disconnected, and so far Mum and Dad hadn't arranged for one that worked in Barbados. Her laptop sat impotently on her table - no broadband yet either.

Everything seemed to take so long in Barbados. Every day Mum would call the phone company and ask if they were going to connect them and every day they said the same thing. 'Maybe tomorrow.'

So, apart from using the landline, which was very expensive, or writing a letter, she was cut off from everyone. She felt the separation was too much to bear.

With one last look at the sinking moon, Jasmine buried her face in the pillow and cried herself to sleep.

Chapter Ten

Over the next couple of weeks, the morning routine was the same. Mum and Dad hurriedly ate breakfast while discussing all the things that had to be done that day. Dad was on his mobile all the time talking to contractors....

'When can I have a phone?' demanded Jasmine, when he finally put his down.

'If you ask like that, young lady... never!'

'What about internet connection? I can't contact my friends. It's like I've died. I hate it here. You said it was going to be wonderful, but it's not, it's just hot all the time and nothing happens.'

'When you start school you'll make some friends,' said Mum sympathetically.

'No, I won't. They hate me because I'm English...'

Mum and Dad glanced nervously at each other. They were having problems of their own fitting in with the Bajans. Dave was finding that the workmen resented being told what to do by what they saw as an outsider, even though he was originally born on the island. They felt he was returning to take advantage and make money.

Marcia too had felt animosity at the bank. She had got the prestigious job of IT Manager because of her experience working in a top position in London, and had beaten several local people to the job. She had heard comments and noticed angry looks from some of the bank employees since she started there two weeks ago.

So both parents knew that what Jasmine was saying was not just the imagination of an unhappy twelve-year-old. They looked over at each other in silence. There was little they could say except that it would get better eventually.

In the meantime there was so much to get done that Jasmine was left to her own devices most of the time. She had plenty of hours and days to think about things. However, the more she thought, the unhappier she became.

The atmosphere on the whole island was charged with the excitement of Crop Over. For months, fantastic Carnival costumes had been prepared for the parades and events that would take place. The main event was a huge parade that would weave its way through the streets of Bridgetown, ending in Spring Gardens.

Crop Over was originally a celebration of the end of the sugar-cane season, but it had grown to be a huge Carnival to which thousands of tourists and locals flocked to enjoy music, colourful costumes, dancing and general merrymaking.

Jasmine didn't want to join in with the celebrations and tried as hard as she could to avoid any involvement, but it was hard not to notice the frantic activity as preparations were made.

There were several Crop Over songs which were played constantly. The favourite was 'English Girl, Why y'wanna go home?' and Jasmine thought that if she heard it one more time she would scream. It was everywhere, in cars, on the radio and in shops. Why couldn't they play pop or music from one of her favourite boy bands, she thought.

It seemed that most people had joined a Carnival group and were going to dance along with them in the big parade. But frankly the whole thing bored Jasmine. Dressing up in silly costumes and dancing through the streets was definitely not her thing. However, Mum and Dad seemed to be getting quite excited about Crop Over and insisted on taking her to the big event.

'I don't want to go,' moaned Jasmine. 'It will be boring. Anyway, we never went to the Carnival in London.'

'Well this is different, you'll like it,' insisted Dad. 'Now pick up the cool box and get in the car.'

It seemed the entire population was out on the streets, either watching or taking part in the parade. Jasmine had to admit it was an amazing spectacle, as thousands of people danced past in fantastic costumes.

Even though it was sweltering in the relentless sun, once or twice Jasmine caught herself being taken over by the carnival atmosphere. But she wasn't going to let her mum and dad know.

❖ ❖ ❖

It was a week later and nothing had changed at home.... no phone, no internet and no friends.

Jasmine either hung around the house or walked the half mile down to West Coast Mall to look round the shops or cross the busy road to the beach, where she sat amongst the holiday makers. She watched them sunning themselves or taking rides on the jet skis ridden by young men, who constantly raced up and down the shoreline looking for customers on the hotel beaches. Occasionally a huge cruise ship would appear on the horizon and head majestically towards Bridgetown, where scores of mini-buses were waiting to take the droves of mostly elderly British or American passengers on high-speed tours of the island.

When a ship was in they swarmed everywhere, even to Holetown, where the tour buses stopped to show the tourists the memorial marking the spot where the first British settlers landed in Barbados 400 years ago and built a church.

The next big town up the coast from there was Speighstown, so Jasmine decided to explore it, and took the ten-minute bus ride up the coast.

For the first time since she had arrived in Barbados the sky was clouded over. Dark clouds massed on the horizon and a relatively cool breeze blew off the sea.

Jasmine got off the bus by Port St Charles, and walked along the beach to the huge marina, where dozens of expensive yachts belonging to the owners of the apartments which edged the marina were moored.

The glistening white yachts were lined up next to each other, bobbing gently on the swell. Most of them were hardly used, they were just status symbols for their wealthy owners. A few, however, showed signs of activity. On board, crew members washed down decks or carried out small maintenance jobs. On one or two, the owners sat on board, idly sipping drinks or eating late breakfasts.

Some of the yachts were enormous, others no more than large speedboats. Each had a name painted on the stern in gold letters with the places they came from underneath. *Sea Girl – Nassau; High Life – Miami; Waverider – Bahamas.*

As Jasmine sat on a low wall, watching, she stared disbelievingly at one particular boat moored a few berths away. Its engines were running and the exhaust bubbled and burbled as it bobbed gently. It wasn't a big one, only about twelve metres long. But there was something amazing about it. On its side were the words, *Jasmine - London.* Jasmine laughed out loud to herself. That's just where this Jasmine wants to be, she thought... London. Memories of Michaela, Sam and Rachel swept into her head. What would they be doing now? Probably texting each other and arranging to meet up. Jasmine desperately wished she was with them, enjoying their summer holiday break.

A man aged about forty, wearing grease-smeared overalls on the back of which was written, 'Bajan Yacht Services', came up from below the deck of the yacht. He was on his mobile phone. 'Wesley here, Mr Tabor, she's running sweet now.... good for another five thousand miles.' As he spoke in his thick Bajan accent, he picked up a toolbox and jumped off the boat on to the wooden jetty. 'OK, I'll just put my tools in the van and I'll meet you by the gate. Yeah, a cheque is fine, no problem.' He walked past Jasmine without noticing her, and hurried along the walkway towards a small blue van.

Suddenly a mad, crazy thought jumped into Jasmine's head. England was four thousand miles away and the man had said the boat could travel for five thousand miles... She glanced at the man, who was now busy chatting to an affluent-looking character who had appeared next to the van.

Jasmine slipped off the wall and, keeping low, she crept towards the boat. Two ropes held it against the jetty, one at the front and the other at the back. They were just looped over the short metal posts on the jetty.

Jasmine eased off the front one and threw the rope on to the deck. Then she did the same with the rear one, jumping neatly on board at the same time. She quickly went to the front seat, where a large steering wheel was surrounded by dials, gauges and a lit-up screen, while the engines gurgled away.

It all looked terrifyingly confusing, but she had seen people driving boats loads of times in films and on TV. She remembered that the big handle next to the steering wheel was what made it go forward.

She sat in the big leather seat and carefully pushed the lever forward. Instantly the engines responded and the low burbling turned to a rumble as the boat moved forward.

Immediately in front was another jetty with more boats moored. Jasmine turned the steering wheel to the right, and the boat reacted. The two men had still not realised what was going on and continued to chat, unaware that the boat was on the move.

Ahead was the narrow entrance to the marina, and beyond – the open sea. Jasmine pointed the front of the boat between the concrete posts and gently pushed the lever further forward. The engine note rose slightly and the boat started to accelerate towards the gap.

This was when the two men realised what was happening. Shouting madly, they sprinted along the road beside the jetty, waving their arms frantically at Jasmine.

She glanced over to her left. The two men were running full speed towards the end of the harbour wall which the boat had to pass before it was in the open sea. People in the nearby boats stood up to get a better look, and others came out on to the balconies which overlooked the marina. Jasmine hadn't thought she would attract so much attention, but it was too late to turn back now.

She realised the boat would pass within a metre or so of the wall, and that it would be possible for someone to jump on to it from the wall if they got there in time. So she pushed the lever all the way forward and instantly the front of the boat lurched upwards.

The engine note changed to a roar and within seconds the boat was passing through the gap and bouncing over the small, choppy waves of the Caribbean sea.

Jasmine looked back and saw the two men still waving frantically at her from the end of the harbour wall. She felt a sense of mad freedom. All her pent-up anger, rage, frustration and unhappiness seemed to blow away in the wind, which buffeted her and pulled at her hair as she sat at the helm of the boat which was going to take her back to England.

She had no idea which direction it was but she didn't care. All she wanted was to get as far away from Barbados as possible!

❖ ❖ ❖

Back in the Marina all hell had broken loose.

The police had arrived and were being told about a crazy young girl who had just stolen a forty-foot sports boat.

Chief Inspector Alleyne, a big man who had been a police officer for twenty years, was finding it hard to believe. But there were at least twenty witnesses who had seen it happen.

Wesley, the service engineer, was standing next to him, looking terrified. 'I could lose my job over this!' he moaned. 'I only turned my back for a minute to speak with Mr Tabor here.'

Mr Tabor, the boat's owner, nodded. 'It all happened so fast, Chief Inspector. She must have been hiding and waiting for her opportunity.'

'Well, she won't get far,' added Wesley. 'I was going to fill the tank with fuel, it's almost empty.'

The first thing Chief Inspector Alleyne did was to alert the coastguards based in Bridgetown, nine miles up the coast, about the incident. They quickly scrambled their big patrol ship, *Trident*, but it was going to take some time to reach them.

A news crew soon arrived from the TV station and were harassing the sweating policeman for a comment.

'We know nothing at the moment,' he said, shaking his head. 'It's too early to comment.'

'Is terrorism involved?' urged the interviewer.

'As far as we know, this is a young girl who has decided to go on a joyride, that's all for now,' he said impatiently.

❖ ❖ ❖

Dave was busy at work. Beside him the radio was playing local music when the DJ interrupted.

'We are just getting news that a young girl has made off with a forty-foot boat which was moored in Port St Charles. The authorities believe the girl is acting alone and the incident is not connected to terrorism. This station will keep you updated on developments....'

'A young girl in a forty-foot boat. She won't get far,' one of the guys commented.'She must be crazy.'

'It's pretty rough out there,' said another, 'and there's a tropical storm brewing. It's that time of the year, man....'

❖ ❖ ❖

Back at the Marina, Chief Inspector Alleyne was shouting angrily into the radio. 'How long before you get here?' he yelled. 'She'll be halfway to St Lucia by the time you catch up with her....'

Just then the news reporter came over and stood agitatedly beside the big police officer.

'I told you, no comment, didn't I?'

The reporter flinched and held out a camcorder. 'I think you should see this, Inspector.'

'Chief Inspector.... What is it?'

'One of the residents grabbed his video camera when he heard all the commotion. He filmed her....'

Alleyne grabbed the camera, his big fingers searching for the play button.... He squinted at the tiny screen... it showed Jasmine at the wheel, the camera zooming in to show her frightened face clearly, as she steered the boat. 'Good Lord! She looks about twelve...

Who the heck is she?'

The reporter shrugged. 'No one round here knows....'

'Can you get this on the midday news?'

'Sure, I'm on my way....'

❖ ❖ ❖

The pictures Jasmine had seen of the Caribbean sea had all shown a beautiful calm expanse of blue water. She looked up at the darkening sky as another vicious wave battered the tiny boat, almost stopping it dead in the water. Plumes of white spray flew over the rails and lashed against the glass of the cabin. The sea was dark green and had a menacing look about it.

The engine note rose and fell, as if it were crying out for respite from the constant demand the sea was making on it.

Jasmine was scared, very scared. She was beginning to realise how stupid and dangerous this stunt was. She looked around, but she could see no land in any direction through the haze of rain that had now started to pummel the roof of the cabin. She began to feel sick. Was it seasickness or fear?

❖ ❖ ❖

Marcia had been busy all morning at the bank. She glanced at her watch. It was just before twelve. Her desk was in an open-plan office behind the cashiers, who sat at the open counter. Beyond them was a waiting area with seats and writing desks for the customers. On the wall was a flat screen TV which was constantly tuned to Channel 8, the local Caribbean Broadcasting Corporation.

Marcia was about to look down at the report she was working on when the news came on with the caption across the screen in big letters. "MARINA DRAMA AS YOUNG GIRL STEALS YACHT."

The next picture on the screen made Marcia jump out of her seat and let out a scream which made everyone in the bank stop in their tracks. Jimmy, the big, fierce-looking security guard, leaped up from the comfy chair in which he spent most of his time, looking round wildly for the cause of Marcia's hysteria.

Marcia was staring in disbelief at the screen on the wall. Everyone turned to see what she was looking at. The picture showed a frozen picture of a young girl sitting at the wheel of a boat. The caption underneath read, 'WHO IS SHE?'

Chapter Eleven

Luther Edwards' calloused left hand gripped the wheel of his thirty-foot fishing boat. He was a tough fisherman who had spent most of his fifty years searching the sea around Barbados for flying fish. His faded baseball cap was on backwards and pulled tightly over his grizzled hair. Not for style, but to keep the wind from plucking it off his head.

His half-closed, amber eyes constantly scanned the sea for telltale signs of a shoal of the elusive, fluttering fish which skipped across the surface, caught in the sunlight like silver birds.

On a good day he could pull in his nets filled to breaking point with a thousand or more of the fifteen-centimetre-long fish. On a bad day he could return home with just a few fish. Today the sea was rough and a tropical storm was moving in fast.

Luther looked up at the clouds and made a mental calculation based on years of experience. Another thirty minutes and it would be too rough to fish, and they would have to turn back empty-handed.

Suddenly the radio burst into life. He fiddled with the ancient set, which squawked and whined until a strong signal came through, and a voice crackled out of the battered speaker.

'Alert. Alert. Coastguard cutter *Trident* on all channels, all shipping please respond, over....'

Luther raised an eyebrow, as he looked at the speaker in surprise. He flicked the transmit switch on the radio. 'Fishing vessel *Freedom* responding. What's the problem? Over.'

'Luther!' the voice came back. 'Where are you?'

Luther recognised the voice of his old friend, Milton Thomas. 'I'm about four miles off Speighstown. It's pretty rough out here. I reckon I'll be heading back in about half an hour. What's going on? Over.'

'Some crazy kid's taken a forty-foot yacht from Port St Charles. She's out there somewhere on her own. Have you seen her?'

'You're kidding me, Milton.'

'I wish I was, Luther... I wish I was.... Keep a look-out and report back if you see her.'

'Will do... but it's getting pretty thick out here. Visibility's next to nothing... Over.' Luther shook his head. He had seen a lot in his time but this was just unbelievable.

He scanned the sea ahead, peering into the haze. Then his sharp eyes picked out a flicker of silver through the spray.

'Devlin! Devlin... get up here, we got a shoal ahead.' He shouted towards a small hatchway below the helm position.

Immediately the head of his son, Devlin Edwards, appeared through the hatch. He was aged about fourteen, but the confident way he swung his lean, muscular body up on to the rolling deck and set about preparing to cast the nets overboard, gave the impression of a much older boy.

Luther pushed the throttle forward, and the noisy, smoking, diesel engine clattered angrily as it pushed the boat towards the scattering fish. It was a routine the two of them had practised many times, and even in the rough sea they got to work. Devlin steadied himself at the side of the boat and waited for his father's command to drop the nets overboard.

Suddenly, without warning, the bucking yacht appeared in front of them like a ghostly mirage. Devlin shouted a warning, but his dad was already spinning the wheel frantically.

The smaller fishing boat lurched and turned sharp

left, almost throwing Devlin overboard, but he reacted fast and stayed on his feet.

Luther watched the white, foam trail left by the yacht as it disappeared into the murk behind him. He spun the wheel in the opposite direction, sending *Freedom* in a wide arc, glancing angrily over his shoulder at the disappearing flickers of silver where the big shoal of fish were swimming, and gave chase.

Jasmine had been going round in circles for the last hour. She had been desperately trying to make the radio work, but the baffling array of switches and dials were too much of a challenge, and now she sat transfixed at the wheel of the yacht, which seemed to have a mind of its own, oblivious to the near miss she'd just had.

Freedom wasn't built for speed and her engine was flat out. Devlin and Luther watched as the yacht gradually pulled away.

Luther flicked the radio switch. 'Fishing vessel *Freedom*, fishing vessel *Freedom* to coastguard cutter *Trident*... come in....'

For a moment all that emitted from the radio was a hiss like water being poured on to red hot metal, then it burst into life with a crackle. 'Coastguard vessel *Trident* responding.... Hi, Luther, what've you got? Over.'

'I got a little girl in a big boat heading south, south-east... Over.'

'We're about seven miles away from you. Can you stop her? Over.'

'She's leaving me behind.... I can't stay with her... Over.'

'We're at full speed - we should be with you in about fifteen minutes....Try to keep her in sight.... Over and out.'

Luther looked up at the darkening sky.... Fifteen minutes was a long time in these conditions. Once the rain really set in and the wind got up, visibility would be down to zero, and without a skilled hand on the wheel of the yacht it could easily flounder and sink.

If Jasmine had been able to understand the meaning of the dials in front of her, she would have seen that the needles on the fuel gauges were flicking on the red section which indicated empty.

A few moments later, first one engine, then the other, spluttered into silence and the boat slowed to a halt. Jasmine felt horribly nauseous.

With the engines silent, the roar of the wind, the lashing of the rain and the thumping of the waves on the hull compounded the stark reality of how serious her situation was.

Her sobs were interrupted by the sound of an engine rising and falling nearby.

Devlin, who had been perched on *Freedom's* bow, staring into the spray, trying to keep sight of the fast-disappearing yacht, suddenly saw it in front to him. He shouted a warning to his father. 'Ease off, Dad!'

Luther cut *Freedom's* engine and let the momentum bring them alongside the yacht. Even in a calm sea it would have been a risky manoeuvre, but in this storm it was plain dangerous. The two vessels were now just a metre apart and the swell was heaving them alarmingly up and down.

Before Luther could stop him, Devlin braced himself and mentally calculated the precise moment to jump. Holding a rope in one hand, he sprang like a cat on to the bucking deck of the yacht. He judged it perfectly, landing squarely in the back of the boat.

Luther breathed a sigh of relief, half angry with his son, half proud of his bravado and skill.

Devlin looked quickly into the cockpit and gave Jasmine a cursory look, shaking his head with exaggerated amazement.

Jasmine looked back, her eyes full of a mixture

of terror and relief.

Before she had a chance to speak Devlin had made his way to the front of the boat and tied the line securely. He signalled with a circular wave to his dad, who had been wrestling to keep the two vessels from crashing into each other.

Luther flung the gearbox into reverse and pulled back until the line went tight. Then, with a quick glance at the compass, he turned *Freedom* back towards Speighstown.

Devlin swung himself into the cabin, his soaking clothes forming an instant puddle on the beige carpet.

Jasmine stared at him sheepishly. She knew he wasn't a policeman or a coastguard, he clearly wasn't old enough to be either. But his confident manner and obvious experience with boats puzzled her.

'I'm sorry,' she blurted out, tears falling from her eyes.

'Why d'ye do it? You got a death wish or somethin'?' demanded Devlin. 'It's dangerous out here. This storm's about to break open big-time.'

'I was going to England,' Jasmine said defensively. 'I would have made it if the petrol hadn't run out.'

Devlin's jaw dropped open in disbelief. Then

he began to laugh uncontrollably, tears running down his cheeks.

'Stop laughing, it's not funny.'

'Are you crazy? Do you know how far it is to England?

'Yes,' answered Jasmine defiantly. 'Four thousand miles.'

'How long do you think that would take you?'

Jasmine gazed at him blankly....

'Well, this thing would only take you two hundred miles, even on a full tank. Anyway, you were heading in the wrong direction. It's that way.' Devlin jerked his thumb over his shoulder.

'I would have made it,' said Jasmine pathetically.

'You have no map... no food, and no idea of how to navigate. And in this weather a boat this small would be smashed to pieces before you got another twenty miles out. If you think it's rough now you aint seen nothin' yet. Oh, and by the way, it's diesel not petrol.'

Jasmine just stared sullenly at the floor.

Devlin went down to the tiny galley and opened the fridge. He pulled out a couple of cans of cola and found some biscuits in the cupboard.

'Here,' he said, a softer note in his voice.

'You must be hungry.'

Jasmine had to agree. She hadn't eaten or drunk anything since breakfast and even though she felt sick from the rocking of the boat, the food and drink were very welcome.

'You're gonna be in big trouble when we get back, y'know.'

'I know...'

'What's yuh name, anyway?'

'Jasmine... Jasmine Braithwaite.'

'Devlin... Devlin Edwards. Braithwaite, that's a Bajan name. But you're English, aren't you?'

'My Dad's from Barbados....' She was interrupted by the deafening foghorn of *Trident*, which blasted above the sound of the rising storm.

The big, grey coastguard-cutter dwarfed the two smaller vessels. Devlin went out to see what was going on, leaving Jasmine to her own thoughts.

She felt stupid and silly. Deep down, she knew she hadn't stood a chance of making it to England, but at least she had tried. Maybe now someone would listen to her.

It took nearly an hour before the coast of Barbados came into view. *Trident* had diverted Luther to the coastguard base in Bridgetown, where Jasmine wwas escorted off the yacht.

Photographers from the local newspaper and a TV camera crew excitedly jostled for pictures of her, as she was led through the pouring rain to the patrol car which was to take her to the police station to meet her parents.

For a second time Dave and Marcia had been put through hell and suffered enormous anxiety because of their daughter's behaviour. So when she arrived at the police station they greeted her with a mixture of immense relief and, understandably, a lot of anger.

Dave had had to drop everything when Marcia called with the news that their daughter had hijacked a luxury yacht. At first Dave thought Marcia had flipped. It was only when one of his workmates rushed in, yelling he had seen Dave's daughter on the TV in the apartment upstairs, that the true magnitude of what Jasmine had done hit him.

After a tearful reunion, Chief Inspector Alleyne took the three of them into his office.

'Sit down, please,' he said, pointing to three wooden chairs arranged round his paper-strewn mahogany desk. He breathed a long sigh as he sank into the large, leather chair on the other side.

Jasmine got the impression he didn't leave that

chair very often and that he was none-too-pleased to have been called out from the comfort of his office to a wet and blustery Port St Charles.

'This is a very serious matter...' he began ominously.

'She didn't mean to cause so much trouble,' Marcia blurted out, holding her damp, white handkerchief to her eye.

The inspector held up his hand up to silence her. 'Your daughter caused a major incident involving the coastguard and the police. Furthermore,' he continued, taking a sheet of paper from the buff-coloured folder on his desk and putting on his reading glasses, 'she endangered the lives of two brave fishermen, Luther Edwards and his son Devlin, who, by the grace of God were in the area and managed to get a line on to the yacht.'

Dave sat with his head in his hands. Marcia just sniffed loudly into her handkerchief, while Jasmine stared out of the window.

She didn't care what happened to her. Nothing could be worse than the feeling of loneliness and anger she felt. She knew there wasn't much they could do to her. Perhaps they would send her home? She crossed her fingers behind her back.

'I'm afraid there will be a hearing in front of the magistrate on Monday. Until then you can go home, but keep an eye on her.... Any more stunts like this and things will get a whole lot worse.' The Chief Inspector stood up, his enormous shoulders almost blocking out the light from the window. He closed the folder and put it on his desk.

Marcia, Dave and Jasmine filed out of his office and went into the street. A clap of thunder introduced more torrents of rain, which lashed down, causing the gutters to turn into miniature rivers, and people to run for cover.

As they drove home, the steam was rising off the hot road. Not much was said. Jasmine just sat sullenly staring out of the window.

They stopped off to pick up a Chefette meal, the Bajan equivalent of a McDonald's, and sat round the kitchen table in an awkward silence eating the rotis, until finally Dave spoke.

'Why did you do it, Jazzie?'

'Why do you think?' retorted Jasmine angrily. 'I told you I want to go home, back to London where all my friends are. I've got no friends here and nothing to do. The kids I've spoken to just laugh at my accent and call me English Girl.'

'Things will change when you go to school, you'll make friends there,' Marcia said hopefully.

'Oh yeah, I've already met some of the so-called friendly kids from Whittington and they weren't exactly falling over themselves to be my 'friends'. I can't even get in touch with my *old* friends at home 'cos of this stupid internet connection.'

'They promised they would connect us soon. I'll give them another call,' said Dave, who was well aware that things didn't move at the same pace as in England. In Barbados things happened in their own time and no amount of cajoling and pestering would get a result. You just had to wait.

'You could have been killed,' Marcia said, her voice shaking. 'Is it worth that? We can work this out if you would just stop being so selfish about it.'

'Selfish! Me, selfish? I didn't ask to be transported to this horrible place. You two just decided for me... and you call me selfish. You two make me laugh.'

'Running away won't make any difference, you know,' said Dad firmly. 'We are here to stay and we have to build a new life, no matter what the adversities.'

Jasmine's eyes flicked up at him. She sensed by the tone in his voice that he was speaking from experience, but she didn't care. 'You can stay here if you like, but as soon as I am old enough I'm going back to London.'

And with that, Jasmine fled to her room and slammed the door behind her.

She knew she had put her parents through hell and deep down she was sorry. But at the same time she was glad. She wanted them to understand just how desperate she was. That will teach them, she thought.

It had been a long, harrowing day and Jasmine quickly fell into a deep sleep from which she didn't wake until the sun was up.

Chapter Twelve

On Monday morning Dave, Marcia and Jasmine sat waiting outside the Magistrates' court in Bridgetown.

Jasmine noticed the man who was the owner of the boat she had stolen talking to Wesley, the engineer, who had left the boat's engines running. They cast an angry look in her direction and moved further away.

Nearby was Luther and his son Devlin. They had been hailed as heroes and their picture had been on the front page of the Advocate, standing proudly next to *Freedom*. However, Luther was none too pleased about being called as a witness, when he could be out fishing.

Devlin saw Jasmine sitting on the bench with her parents and flashed a smile at her.

Jasmine smiled back shyly.

'Is that the boy who saved you?' asked Marcia.

'Yes.'

'Why don't you go over and say hello?'

Jasmine tried to look casual as she got up, and pretended to read the notice-board outside the court.

'How's it goin'?' Devlin was standing behind her, his hands in his pockets.

'OK,' Jasmine muttered, 'considering I'm a criminal.'

They both let out a laugh.

'Yeah, a real bad one too. Piracy doesn't go down too well round here,' he said, trying to look serious. 'They'll probably hang you from the yard arm.'

'I don't care what they do...' said Jasmine despondently.

Just then, Dave came over. 'I haven't had a chance to thank you for what you did. If it hadn't been for you and your dad, well... who knows.'

Devlin looked embarrassed. 'It was nothin',' he said.

'They've called your case, Jasmine, let's go,' said her mother anxiously.

Jasmine felt a slight flutter of nerves as she followed her parents towards the steps leading into the court.

As she was a child, she was asked to sit on a chair at a table in front of the Magistrate, who listened carefully to the facts.

The owner of the boat turned out to be a man from London. He told the court he had at first been very angry about having his boat taken. But as there was no damage to his yacht, after hearing about why she took it and how unhappy she was, his anger had turned to sympathy. So he told the court he did not want to press charges.

The Magistrate gave Jasmine a long lecture about the danger in which she had put herself and lots of other people. She had caused a major alert involving the coastguard, but in the circumstances and on account of the generosity of Mr Tabor, she was prepared to let her off with a severe reprimand. She asked Jasmine to promise to be a good girl in the future and not to do anything foolish like this again.

Marcia and David looked over at their daughter anxiously, awaiting her answer.

Jasmine desperately wanted to say, 'No, I want to go home!' But the look on her parents' faces made her relent. 'Yes, ma'am, I promise,' she replied, bowing her head.

❖ ❖ ❖

In the days that followed, Jasmine kept herself to

herself. Thankfully the broadband connection was in and she finally got a new mobile. So she spent most of her time indoors on Facebook. It was a bit difficult because of the time difference, so no one back in the UK was online when she was.

It was the same with text messages. Michaela, Sam and Rachel were all asleep when Jasmine was trying to contact them. Michaela always answered texts as soon as she could, but Sam tended to forget and Rachel was hopeless at the best of times.

Phoning was out of the question of course, as she would use all her allowance up in no time. Besides, Jasmine began to get the distinct impression that her friends in England were preoccupied with their own lives. She hoped they were not forgetting about her.

Chapter Thirteen

At last the summer holidays ran out and the schools re-opened.

The previous week, Jasmine and her mother had gone into Bridgetown and bought the last bits and pieces of uniform and school paraphernalia. Jasmine was feeling very nervous about starting a new school, and kept having mini panic attacks as they negotiated their way along the crowded pavement.

'I hate this stupid uniform,' she complained, holding up the long, shapeless, khaki dress they'd just bought.

Marcia tried to stay upbeat. 'I think it's rather nice,' she said.

'Well, you wear it, then,' snapped Jasmine. 'I hate going to new schools.'

'It will be the same as last year back in England when you had to start at Jibson School,' Mum pointed out. 'You met new people there, so it shouldn't be too difficult this time.'

'But this is different. We're in a foreign country now,' sulked Jasmine. 'Anyway, I did know some people who went to Jibson.'

'But you wouldn't have known anyone if you had gone to St Gabriel's, which was top of your list. No one from your school was going there.'

Jasmine couldn't be bothered to argue about the same old thing again. She was too hot, and to make matters worse, another deluge of rain sent everyone running for cover.

'And to think we used to complain about the rain in England,' laughed her mum, putting up her umbrella.

❖ ❖ ❖

A week later Jasmine found herself standing at the gates of Whittington School.

The school stood on a hill. The two-storey, pink-painted, colonial buildings clustered round a central area with benches and pathways bordered by flowering shrubs and tall trees. The rear of the buildings was surrounded by a vast expanse of playing fields, including cricket pitches, tennis courts and an athletics track. The whole compound was enclosed by a white wall.

A wide entrance was protected by two elaborately crested wrought-iron gates, emblazoned with the words *Education is your Passport to Life* in large, gold letters. Beside the gates was a sign that read *Whittington School, Established 1820, Barbados Ministry of Education*.

The school was very proud of its heritage and long list of illustrious past pupils. It had been originally established to educate the children of the white plantation owners, but it was now a free school, open to all Bajans.

Dave had registered Jasmine at the school long before she had arrived in Barbados to make sure she had a place. Jibson School had sent reports of her grades to show she had reached the high standard necessary to be accepted. He had chosen the school for its high academic reputation.

The first day was a bewildering series of events, starting with a long lecture from the Principal, Dr Cedric Mortimer, a tall, bespectacled man with a high, shiny, ebony forehead.

He stood on the raised stage behind a lectern, his flowing blue-and-black academic robes over a dark suit. 'Welcome to a new school year here at

Whittington, and especially to our new pupils. You are following in the footsteps of many great alumni. We have a long and distinguished record of producing outstanding individuals here at Whittington.' He droned on in his strong Bajan accent, reeling off a long list of names, none of which meant anything to Jasmine.

She sat bewildered in the large assembly hall with its highly polished, mahogany, parquet floor, which reflected the light from the tall, arched windows. Above her was a narrow balcony, which stretched around the entire hall. This was where the older students sat and looked down on the assembly below. Above them was a high ceiling from which hung ten large chandelier lights and four slowly rotating fans.

Jasmine looked round curiously at her fellow students. The girls mostly wore their hair neatly plaited, and decorated with dark blue ribbons. They wore khaki dresses, regulation belts with school colours, navy-blue ankle socks and formal, black, flat-heeled shoes with laces. The boys wore open-necked khaki shirts, khaki shorts, plain black belts, navy blue knee-high socks with gold hose tops and black formal shoes with laces

After being lectured for what seemed like ages,

they filed outside and stood in groups, waiting for the teachers to come out and take them to their classes. So far no one had spoken to Jasmine and she stood alone in the shade of a tree, trying to look as if she didn't care.

She noticed people staring at her, but as soon as she looked at them they turned their eyes quickly away. She noticed the girls she had met on the beach, Maxine and Josie, looking over at her and giggling with a group of other girls. She looked amongst the boys, trying to pick out Breezy and Broderick.

'Hello, English girl,' came a voice from behind her. She turned and saw Breezy and Broderick, who had sneaked up silently.

'Hello,' Jasmine replied, feeling relieved that at least someone was talking to her.

'How you gettin' on?' smiled Breezy

'All right,' lied Jasmine.

'Which form you in?' Broderick smirked.

'2B... Mrs Dalgleish.'

'Me too,' said Breezy with a note of satisfaction in his voice, winking at Broderick. His eyes momentarily flickered and refocused over Jasmine's shoulder.

Jasmine turned round to see what had caused him to hesitate.

'Talkin' to your little English girl again, Breezy... you got a thing for her?' sneered Maxine. The group of girls surrounding her giggled uncontrollably.

Breezy looked embarrassed. Jasmine got the impression Breezy was not as sure of himself as he made out, and that Maxine was in control here.

'No... no, I was just talkin', that's all,' he stammered. 'C'mon, Brod.' He swaggered off towards a group of boys, closely followed by Broderick.

Maxine and her gang moved in closer. 'I see you on the TV... thief a boat to get back to England. How stupid is that?' She gave Jasmine another of her disdainful looks before spinning on her heel and sauntering off, followed by her cronies.

Jasmine was speechless. What has this girl got against me? she wondered.

Just then the bell rang and everyone lined up in neat rows according to which class they had been assigned to. Jasmine had received a letter telling her she would be in class 2B and that her form teacher would be Mrs Dalgleish.

To her dismay, Jasmine found herself in the same line as Maxine and Breezy. Josie and Broderick were in the next line, 2A.

As they stood in the hot sun, out of the shade of

the trees, there was much giggling and face pulling. Then, on the stroke of nine, an army of teachers emerged from the staff-room entrance. The male teachers mostly wore darks suits with collar and ties and the women were in smart clothes.

Four women came over to where Jasmine's year was lined up, and stood facing them. Nothing was said, but the unruly kids fell silent. Something in the teachers' demeanour just said, 'Don't mess!'

Mrs Dalgleish, head of the Second Year, was a stocky, stern woman aged about 45. She wore her hair pulled back in a tight bun, and a pair of gold-rimmed glasses sat on the end of her nose. Her crisp, white blouse was tucked firmly into a beige, pleated skirt, and her brown brogues were polished and tightly laced.

She viewed her new class over her glasses, like an artist assessing the material she had to work with this year, noting what would be needed to get the best from them.

The other three teachers did much the same with their charges.

Mrs Thomas was at the head of 2A. She was a strikingly tall woman with a straight, dancer's back. Her mouth looked as if it had never experienced a smile.

Mrs Crozier was an athletic, sporty type with muscular shoulders and a cat-like gracefulness in her step. Jasmine could sense a steely air of determination in her and was sure it would be foolish to get on the wrong side of her. She, unsurprisingly, was head of sports for the Lower School.

Miss Groves, 2D, was the youngest teacher, and looked more approachable. Her hair was shiny and straightened. It hung plainly down the sides of a pleasant face from which shone a pair of mischievous, twinkling eyes. She reminded Jasmine a little of Miss Vine back in England, and Jasmine wished she was in her class.

As soon as Mrs Dalgleish was satisfied the new classes were giving her and her colleagues their full attention she simply clapped her hands and said, 'Follow your teachers to your classrooms.'

Each of the four lines marched off behind their respective teachers into the pink-coral, stone building.

Jasmine walked with a sense of foreboding in her heart. She had a bad feeling about this. School back in London had been quite a fun place and the teachers were on the whole quite easy-going, and often engaged in a bit of banter and chat with the pupils. But this lot looked as if the word 'fun' was not in their vocabulary.

Her fears were confirmed when they sat down for their first lesson. The atmosphere was serious and studious, and talking was kept to a minimum.

The rest of the morning was taken up with copying timetables and getting text books. Jasmine carefully wrote everything into her timetable book as Mrs Dalgleish listed each day's lessons. But she had a bit of trouble understanding some of the words Mrs Dalgleish used and her strong Bajan accent.

Without thinking, Jasmine said in a loud voice, 'Er, hold on, Miss, can you say that again?'

Mrs Dalgleish stopped talking and stared at her in disbelief, and the rest of the class froze as if time had suddenly stopped.

'What is your name, young lady?' Mrs Dalgleish asked in a measured tone.

'Jasmine Braithwaite,' Jasmine said quietly.

'Jasmine Braithwaite,' repeated Mrs Dalgleish, as if trying to secure it in her memory. 'I understand you originate from the United Kingdom.'

Jasmine nodded nervously.

'Well, here in Barbados it is not the convention to

speak to a teacher without first raising your hand and waiting to be acknowledged. Is that quite clear?'

'Yes, Miss,' said Jasmine, feeling the eyes of the class on her.

'Oh and in future you will address me as Ma'am. Now, where were we…?'

Jasmine's face burned and she wanted the floor to open up and swallow her, she felt so humiliated. This was going to give Maxine and her gang yet more ammunition.

The next few days were taken up with getting used to the routine at school and Jasmine tried to keep her head down. Many of the students looked at her and sniggered, calling her Captain Scarlet because of her boat-stealing adventure.

Any hopes of making friends with anyone seemed impossible. It seemed as though there was an invisible barrier between her and the Bajan kids. They looked at her as some kind of oddity – an outsider, a foreigner, an interloper – who was intruding on their lives.

Most Bajans could put up with visitors to the island. After all, tourism was their life-blood, and a major proportion of the people made their living from it. But there seemed to be a big difference between visiting for a holiday and moving to the island permanently.

Every morning Jasmine got a sick feeling in her stomach as she walked the mile or so to school.

Maxine Pendergrass was the main culprit. Her sneering distain and constant digs were relentless. She was a clever manipulator and managed to turn the others against Jasmine. Breezy tried to make conversation, but he was always looking over his shoulder, fearing Maxine would spot him talking to her.

Jasmine was miserable and lonely, and she ached for a friend. She sat at the back of the class by herself, gazing out of the window, looking up at the planes high above. She wished she could fly away too, like the tourists going back to England.

Why did she have to be here?

Chapter Fourteen

Dave wasn't able to spend much time at home with Jasmine and Marcia. He was too busy making sure the building works were on target. He had been on-site all the time, working night and day since he had landed the big contract with O'Brien.

It was a sore point, giving new contracts to what the Bajans saw as outsiders. But it was because there was so much development going on in Barbados. If you wanted a job finished on time, the only way to do it was to hire foreign contractors as well as the locals.

The locals didn't like it, but they had to put up with it, and they tended to give people like Dave a hard time. He constantly had to cajole them to work faster – but that just wasn't the Bajan way.

The developer for whom Dave was working was an Irishman by the name of O'Brien, who had made a fortune building luxury homes and apartments.

Dave had persuaded him he could do a good job, and had got the contract with a promise of more work if the job was completed on time and under budget.

O'Brien was friendly with another developer called Carlton Harrison, who some said was able to smooth the way when it came to planning consent. He had friends in high places.

The daily newspaper, the Advocate, was always running stories on Harrison, writing about his shady dealings and calling for investigations into how he made his money. So Dave was surprised when, out of the blue, he got a call on his mobile from Mr Harrison.

'Dave, Carlton Harrison here, I want you to come over to my place for a drink tonight. I'd like to talk to you about a proposition.' Before Dave could reply, Harrison went on. 'Make it nine o'clock, my place is up by the polo field.'

'OK,' answered Dave, looking at the phone in puzzlement.

'What does he want?' said Marcia, unpacking the shopping.

'I really don't know,' said Dave slowly, 'something about a proposition.'

'Well, you'd better go… It may be more work.'

'I will,' said Dave. 'I'll have a shower and go straight off.'

Harrison's home was a huge plantation-style house, set back from the road with a high, coral stone wall around it. The metal gate swung open when Dave gave his name to the metallic voice that came from the speaker.

Dave's scruffy pick-up truck looked out of place parked in front of the immaculate, two storey house, also built from beautiful, pink-tinged coral stone.

The ornate front door swung open and a suited man stepped forward into the glow of the floodlights that bathed the house in orange light. 'Mr Harrison is expecting you, this way please,' he said, bowing slightly.

The hallway was wide and its smooth, marble floor was polished to perfection. Expensive paintings and sculptures were all over the place.

The man in the suit, who Dave guessed must be some kind of butler, led him through the house and out on to a terrace lit again by orange floodlights. There were several big, comfy sofas and low, glass coffee tables with vases of flowers on them. To one side there was a bar, with four high chairs and dozens of bottles of drink lined up on glass shelves.

Beyond a low wall was a large swimming pool, which glowed with a magical, blue shimmer from the underwater lights. The butler gestured towards the bar. 'Would Sir like a drink? Mr Harrison will be out in a moment.'

'Coke, please,' said Dave absently. It took quite a lot to phase him but he had to admit this was impressive.

'Daaave', came the voice of Carlton Harrison. Dave turned and saw Harrison, dressed in a pink polo shirt and white cotton trousers, standing with a drink in his hand.

He was surprisingly small, about five foot four and slightly built. But he had a weasel-like face which showed cunning and determination even through his smile.

'Dave...so good of you to come. Hopkins sort you out with a drink? Good. Now, I'll come straight to the point, Dave.... Your property, it's in a prime position down on the coast road....What is it, a couple of acres?'

'Just under,' replied Dave.

'Yes, yes,' nodded Harrison, as if Dave's answer was not relevant. 'The thing is,' he went on, 'I'd like to take it off your hands. I'll give you a fair price for it and even give you the contract for the kitchen and bathroom work.'

Dave spluttered on his Coke. This was the last thing he'd been expecting. 'I didn't think a small plot like mine would be of interest,' he said.

'Normally it wouldn't be,' said Harrison, 'but your place is in an ideal position and has great potential.'

'Look, Mr Harrison,' said Dave, putting his drink down.

'Carlton, please,' smiled Harrison.

'Er, look, Carlton, that house and land has been in my family since the days of slavery. It's part of the reason my family and I moved back to Barbados. I spent months doing up the house. To be honest I've got no intention of selling. Anyway, it's not mine to sell yet. It still belongs to my mother.'

Harrison's face twitched slightly with irritation but he quickly regained his composure. 'Dave... I don't think you understand. That bit of land is prime property. I'm offering you a small fortune for it. I can get twenty apartments on there and a couple of townhouses. I'm sure you can persuade your dear old mother to sell.'

'What makes you think I couldn't do the development myself?' said Dave.

Harrison laughed. 'Well, you could, if you can raise the ten million dollars it would cost to build it, and get the plans through. Don't forget, Dave, I've been at this game a long time.' He gave an expansive wave around the terrace and pool area as if to make his point. 'It would take you years even to get started. I could start work there in three months.'

Dave was beginning to get annoyed. He didn't like the way this man was treating him as if he were an idiot. He knew full well how hard it was to get things done in Barbados, unless you had the right connections, that is. And he knew what his land was worth. But he had never considered developing it because he, like many others, felt there was already too much development and that many historic parts of Barbados were fast disappearing. There had been a house on that plot for over two hundred years and for much of that time it had been in the Braithwaite family.

'I'm sorry, Mr Harrison, I'm not interested,' he said firmly. 'That land is going to stay as it is, as long as I'm alive.'

Harrison was staring at Dave with fury in his eyes. 'You might regret that decision. Why don't you think about it?' he said, before turning on his heel and disappearing back inside the house.

Dave drove home faster than he should have

done, feeling angry and upset. He wasn't going to be pushed around by Harrison, but he was worried he had made a powerful enemy, and he felt sure that this wasn't going to be his last encounter with him.

Chapter Fifteen

The arrangement for Jasmine to hop on the bus over to Grannie Braithwaite's after school was working well. Every day, the bus dropped her at a place known as the Soup Bowl, right on the beach in the centre of Bathsheba.

One day, a week after Dave's encounter with Mr Harrison, Jasmine got off the bus and looked out at the raging Atlantic Ocean. The ever-present wind whipped her hair and the salty spray stung her eyes.

For some reason, today, instead of going up the hill towards Grannie Braithwaite's house, she walked slowly down to the water's edge.

Grannie Braithwaite had told her that Britain was four thousand uninterrupted miles from where she was standing. She had also told her stories of the enslaved Africans who had thrown themselves into the raging waves, believing they would be taken home by the sea. Jasmine stared at the breakers further out at sea. A few intrepid surfers were determinedly paddling their boards. Occasionally one of them caught a wave and stood upright for a tantalising few moments, before falling back into the swirling water.

It was a notoriously dangerous area and there were signs warning that only the most experienced and capable swimmers should venture into the water. There had been many cases of people drowning here in the vicious undercurrents.

Jasmine wondered what it would be like to drown, to sink below the water and slowly slide into the indigo depths, life slowly leaving your body and darkness closing over you like a blanket. She put her foot on to the wet sand at the water's edge and allowed the wave to engulf it, soaking her shoe and sock.

The water tugged at her foot as the wave receded back down the beach. Maybe this was the answer, she thought. Perhaps it would be for the best, the best for everyone. No one would miss her, and her parents wouldn't have to worry about her any more. She took a step forward, and this time another wave closed round both her feet. She felt the urge to let it pull her into the sea.

Suddenly her thoughts were interrupted by the noise of footsteps behind her on the stony beach.

She looked round and saw four boys standing, staring at her. They were wearing school uniform, but she didn't recognise which school it was.

'What – what do you want?' she said, her heart accelerating to double speed.

'You dat crazy English girl who steal d'boat... aren't you?' He was a tall, well-built boy, about fourteen. His two comrades were smaller and skinnier and stood round him like stooges.

'Yeah, you're crazy!' one of them chirped up.

'What you doin' round here? We don't want your kind... go back to England where you belong.'

'Look at her in her Whittington school uniform, a school for losers. We hate your lot.'

The first boy reached down and picked up her bag before she could grab it. 'What have we here?' he said, holding it up above his head.

'Give it back to her, Harrison!'

Jasmine spun round to see where the voice came from. The sun was low in the sky and she could just make out a figure standing silhouetted against the sea. But the voice was familiar. It was Devlin.

At first she hardly recognised him in his school uniform. It was the same one as the three boys. Somehow she had not imagined him as a schoolboy.

'Well, if it isn't Fish Boy. Come to save the English girl again. You're making a habit of it. I hope she likes the smell of fish....' sneered Harrison.

'Do you enjoy picking on girls, Harrison? Why don't you try picking on me instead?'

Harrison flicked a glance at his two cronies but they were looking away. 'Shouldn't you be out fishing or something?' he taunted.

'Get lost, Harrison,' Devlin said menacingly.

'I can make things very difficult for you, Edwards. My dad can speak to the licensing people about your dad's wreck of a boat. It's not fit to be on the sea. My dad's boat will slice it in half one of these days.'

Devlin took a step towards Harrison, his hand tightening into a fist.

Harrison backed away, trying to look tough before turning and swaggering off. 'See you around, Fish Boy!' he shouted, without turning round.

'Thanks, Devlin... again,' said Jasmine.

'Think nothin' of it,' he shrugged. 'That Ronnie Harrison is a creep like his rich father. His dad's boat, the *Barracuda*, is always messing up the fishing round here. It's one of those big racing speedboats, built for show-offs. It occasionally comes over this side of the island. I can't think why, all the show-offs are on the West Coast.'

Suddenly Jasmine made the connection. 'Harrison! Is he the son of Carlton Harrison?'

'Yep.'

'My dad had a run-in with him last week. He's not very nice.'

'He's a big shot in Barbados, which is why Ronnie pushes people around and thinks he can get away with the things he does. But I can handle him.'

Jasmine and Devlin walked slowly along the beach for a while, in silence.

'What you doin' over this side of the island?' he finally asked.

'My grannie lives just up the road from here.'

'You mean old Mrs Braithwaite?'

'Yes, she takes care of me after school.'

'I think she knows my dad. So, you a real Bajan,' he teased.

'I was born in London.'

'I'm gonna go to London one day,' Devlin said dreamily. 'What's it like there?'

It didn't take much encouragement from Devlin to get Jasmine talking about London. 'Oh, it's awesome. There's so much to do. Me and my friends used to go shopping in the mall.'

'Like West Coast Mall?' chipped in Devlin.

'No, it's huge... massive, with designer shops. The streets are really busy, full of cars and buses. And millions and millions of people everywhere.'

'What, like Bridgetown?' said Devlin.

Jasmine laughed loudly. 'About a thousand times bigger. The buses are great big, red double-deckers. And then there's the underground.'

Devlin's eyes widened. 'Underground!'

'Yeah, the trains go through tunnels under the streets. It's really cool, you just go down to the station on an escalator and come up somewhere else. It's brilliant.' Devlin was trying to imagine an underground train, but Jasmine rushed on. 'Then there's the weather... most of the time it's freezing cold or raining.'

'Or snowing?' Devlin interrupted. 'I've seen snow in films and magazines. What's it really like?'

'Well, it doesn't snow that often. I've only seen it a few times but when I did it was so awesome. And then everyone stops working.'

'You mean they go on strike?'

'No, silly, just the trains and cars and buses can't go, so they cancel everything. It's a real mess and then everybody complains on the TV news.'

'I wouldn't complain,' said Devlin. 'I'd love to play snowballs like they do in the movies.'

'Well, one day maybe you'll see it for yourself. I just wish I was there right now,' sighed Jasmine.

They stopped at the end of the beach where the road curved upwards towards the clump of houses where Grannie Braithwaite lived.

'Well, I've got to get back to help my dad. He's working on the boat. She needs a lot of attention at her age!'

'Thanks again,' smiled Jasmine. 'I'll be here on Sunday. We're all going to church with Grannie Braithwaite. Will you and your dad be there?

'No,' said Devlin flatly. 'We don't go to church. Not since my mother died seven years ago.... My dad says God shouldn't have let her die.'

'Do you feel the same way, Devlin?' Jasmine asked. 'I mean about God.'

Devlin shrugged, 'I don't know. My mother was great. When she died I was seven and I cried for two weeks. Reverend Rock, at the church, says it's easy to blame God when you lose someone you love... "The Lord take her away because he needed her in heaven," he said. I told him I needed her here.'

Jasmine's heart lurched with sympathy. 'It must

have been awful losing your mother,' she said softly, trying to hold back a tear.

'Yeah, it was.'

'I know how it feels,' said Jasmine

'How can you know?' Devlin asked incredulously.

'I had a little brother, but he died when he was only five months old. I don't know why he was taken away, he was so tiny.'

Devlin didn't say anything, but Jasmine pretended not to notice him roughly wipe away the single tear that rolled down his cheek.

They turned off the beach and walked slowly up the steep hill which led to Grannie Braithwaite's house. They stopped at the gate, an awkward silence falling between them.

Then Grannie Braithwaite called from the kitchen window. 'Hello, Devlin, how's your father these days? I haven't seen him in church for such a long while.'

Devlin jumped at the sound of her voice, almost standing to attention. 'He's OK, thanks,' he replied politely, becoming more boyish when speaking to an elder.

'Give him my best, won't you?' said Grannie Braithwaite, with just a hint of sternness in her voice.

'Yes, Ma'am,' said Devlin, looking slightly nervous. 'I gotta go now,' he said, turning to Jasmine. 'Got work to do. See you around. Bye.' After about twenty paces he turned and looked back, to see if she was still there.

He waved another goodbye and moved off towards Tent Bay, the small harbour where his dad would be waiting for him to help unload the day's catch and prepare *Freedom* for the next morning.

Grannie Braithwaite was sitting in her usual chair on the veranda, and she smiled warmly as Jasmine clumped up the wooden steps. 'I see you made a friend. That young Devlin's a good boy. You seem to like him, am I right?'

Jasmine felt her face flush with embarrassment. 'He's all right.' She shrugged nonchalantly.

'I knew his mother, bless her soul. She died of the cancer, y'know.'

Jasmine sat down next to Grannie Braithwaite. 'Do you think God decides when you're going to die, or can you decide for yourself?'

'Well, that's a seriously big question, Jasmine. I have always believed that everything happens for a reason. It may not be clear what the reason is when it's happening, and things that happen might not suit you. But darlin', they happen and you just have to trust in the Lord, cos He knows best.'

Grannie Braithwaite smiled lovingly at Jasmine as she ran her soft hand over her forehead. It made Jasmine feel so much better and somehow took away the feeling of unhappiness that she felt deep in her heart. 'I know how you are feelin', Jasmine. Barbados can be a difficult place to get used to. The people are funny about what they see as 'outsiders' coming to take away what belongs to them.'

'They keep on calling me the English Girl,' said Jasmine, leaning back and closing her eyes in exasperation.

'They used to call me that too, y'know,' laughed Grannie Braithwaite.

Jasmine opened her eyes with a start. 'You?' she exclaimed. 'I don't understand. Why?'

Grannie Braithwaite laughed again. 'Of course, you don't know the story, do you?'

Jasmine shook her head.

'Well, when I was a young girl I went to England, on a big ship. At the time there were lots of advertisements in the papers asking for people to go there and work to rebuild the country after the war. I had trained as a nurse and they were asking for nurses, so I decided to go and see what it was all about.'

Jasmine sat staring at Grannie Braithwaite, her mouth open in amazement. 'Why didn't Dad tell me this?' she asked.

'Well, he was probably going to. Wait here. I've got something you might like to see.'

Grannie Braithwaite got up and went inside the house, returning a moment later with a battered cardboard box. She sat down again, placing the box on her lap and putting her reading glasses on. Then she opened the lid and took out a pile of old black-and-white photographs whose edges were turning brown.

'This is me. I was about eighteen there. Look, you can see the other passengers on the ship.'

Jasmine looked at the fading picture. It showed a beautiful, young, black girl wearing a pretty, white dress. Her hair was straightened and she wore a small, pillbox hat and white gloves. Jasmine could just make out the face of her grannie, only not old. She was standing on what appeared to be the deck of a ship and in the background were other people.

The girls were all dressed in a similar way to Grannie Braithwaite, and the men wore smart suits with baggy trousers and double-breasted jackets.

Underneath they wore white shirts and wide patterned ties.

'And this one here is me as a nurse.' The picture showed the beautiful young girl again, this time in a crisp uniform.

'Wow, Grannie B, you were beautiful!'

'What do you mean, were?'

Jasmine laughed, 'Sorry, Grannie B....'

'No, I know what you mean. In those days I was young and beautiful. But it was hard, not just for me, but for all the others who went up to England to work. I booked my passage like everyone else who wanted adventure and a new life. My father didn't want me to go but I was headstrong and determined. The journey took two weeks on the ship, and for the first four days I was so seasick.'

'That must have been terrible, Grannie B.'

'It was. But then I got used to it and started to enjoy the journey. The ship picked up passengers from Trinidad, Grenada and St Lucia before reaching Barbados. So it was exciting meeting new people from the different Caribbean islands. When we started to get closer to England we noticed a chill in the air and none of us were prepared for the cold. We arrived in Southampton on 2nd October, 1956.

I remember it as if it were yesterday. And I can tell you, my dear, my teeth were chattering and not just from the freezing cold. I had never imagined anything like it.'

'You must have been scared, Grannie B.'

'Oh, things got a whole lot worse, I can tell you. All I had was a ticket and a piece of paper with the address of the hospital I was to start work at in Norwich.'

'Norwich!' exclaimed Jasmine.

'That's right, I had to find my way from Southampton to Norwich all by myself. And in those days there was no interweb or mobile phones to help, like you people have these days.'

'Inter*net*, Grannie B.'

'Whatever you call it! Anyway, I made it somehow and started work as a junior nurse, even though my qualifications were better. That first winter was the worst I can remember. I was so cold I nearly froze to death. We all slept in a dormitory and we had just one blanket each. We had to be up at six in the morning and work all day, six days a week.'

'That's terrible, why didn't you go on strike?'

'Oh, you didn't do things like that then. You just carried on. Anyway, I had other problems to deal with. You see, there weren't many people like me in Norwich at the time and...'

'You mean black people?'

'Yes, although they called us coloured people or negroes then, well, the nice ones did. The others called us terrible names. Lots of the patients in the hospital refused to have us touch them. And when I became a district nurse some of the people I had to visit wouldn't let me in their houses.'

'But that's racist! They should have been arrested or something.'

'It wasn't against the law in those days, sweetheart. Anyway, we just got on with life and tried to ignore the insults and the way we were treated. Many people had sold everything to pay for their passage to England. There was no way back for them. They couldn't just get on a bus and go home.'

'But you came back, didn't you, Grannie B?'

'Yes, I did, after twenty years. During that time I met your Grandad Irving. He had been in the British army during the war, fighting for King and country, the British Empire. But when the war was over he was the same as all of us. He was insulted and called names, even though he had fought bravely for Britain and nearly died.

That really hurt him. He never got over it. The rejection stayed with him for the rest of his life. One day, out of the blue, he said to me, "Let's go home, Veronica. I've had enough." And I said, "Yes, let's." The funny part of it was that when I told the hospital I was going, they begged me to stay. The patients eventually showed they loved me. Funny that, wasn't it?'

'I'll bet you were glad to get home, Grannie B,' said Jasmine, enthralled.

'Well that's another funny part of the story.' Grannie Braithwaite smiled wistfully. 'You see, it works both ways, because when I came home the people here gave me and Irving a hard time. Some of them accused us of being failures. They had heard the streets of London were paved with gold and life there was great. No one had told them the truth, because Caribbean people were too proud to admit how horrible it was. So they thought we had given up and come home with our tails between our legs. Others accused us of being traitors and deserting our island to go off to England. They would say, "Go back to England, we don't want you here!"'

'That's what they say to me, Grannie B,' said Jasmine. 'Like I said, they call me English Girl all the time.'

Grannie Braithwaite laughed. 'Well, nothin's changed. That's what they called me too, because I had picked up English mannerisms and a bit of the accent. That was in 1976 and your dad was seven. He stayed here until he was 18, then he went to England to study. And that's where he met your mother. So now you know a bit about your roots, and I'm going to have to tell you more another time, darlin'.'

Jasmine looked at Grannie Braithwaite in a new way. She couldn't imagine how she had been through all this, and yet still seemed so loving and kind, with no hatred or bitterness in her heart.

'Look at the time. I'd better get you something to eat,' said Grannie Braithwaite, standing up. 'Your dad will soon be here to pick you up.'

Jasmine was amazed to see that the sun had dropped towards the horizon, and the sound of the crickets had got louder, as it always did at dusk. Time seemed to have stood still while Grannie Braithwaite told her story.

Chapter Sixteen

That evening Dad was late picking Jasmine up. He had a distant look on his face and didn't say much. It was clear he had something on his mind.

When they got home, Jasmine went to her room to finish an essay, but she could hear her parents talking loudly in the living room. She got up from her desk and stood by her door.

'He can't do that!' said her mother, her voice sounding angry.

'Well, he just did,' replied Dad. 'It's obvious what's happened. That crook Carlton Harrison has put pressure on O'Brien to get rid of me because I won't sell this land to him.'

'But O'Brien doesn't have to do what Harrison says, does he?'

'Everyone has to go through Harrison. He has a lot of influence in the planning department. He can make it impossible for O'Brien to build anything on the island.'

'Surely people know Harrison is a crook. Why doesn't someone report him?'

'Everyone knows, but even the newspapers can't pin anything on him. He's clever enough to cover his tracks. What they need is some hard evidence of his dirty dealings.'

'But you've got a contract with O'Brien.'

'I know, but unfortunately there's a clause saying if the work isn't on schedule he can cancel the contract, and as you know I'm falling behind. I just can't get the work done fast enough. The men will only work at their own speed. So he's got an excuse to get rid of me if he wants to. I'll just have to keep on going and see what happens. I've got to get this job done, otherwise we're finished.'

Jasmine went back to her work. In her heart she felt guilty because she was glad that it was all going wrong for her parents. She felt like confronting them and saying, 'I told you so. We should have stayed in England, then none of this would be happening.'

She wondered whether, if things got any worse, they would decide to go back to England. It was a glimmer of hope. This, coupled with the chance meeting with Devlin and the conversation with Grannie B, lifted Jasmine's spirits so that she faced the daily terror of school with a bit more courage. It was still a miserable experience, though.

Suzanne Thomas, one of the few white girls in the school, occasionally smiled at Jasmine and made an effort to speak to her when Maxine wasn't around.

Jasmine suspected that she only hung out with Maxine and her crowd to avoid being picked on by them. At first she thought Suzanne was English, and that might be a reason to form a friendship. But it turned out she was a white Bajan, and she spoke in a broad Bajan accent which always surprised Jasmine, no matter how often she heard it. Each morning before the bell went, Jasmine would sit under the tree while Maxine and her group of cronies stood nearby, throwing dirty looks her way and bursting into shrieks of laughter every time Maxine spoke.

One morning, while Jasmine sat with her head deep in a book, she felt someone sit beside her. She looked round and saw it was Suzanne Thomas. She was on her own.

'Where's Maxine?' asked Jasmine, looking around.

'I dunno, she's gone off somewhere. What you readin'?' she asked.

'*Jonathan Livingstone Seagull*,' replied Jasmine.

'What's it about?'

'A seagull called Jonathan Livingstone, who overcomes all adversities. My gran gave it to me.'

'Mmm, I like love stories.... Crisp?'

She held out a bag of crisps and Jasmine gingerly took one, half expecting her to snatch the bag away at the last second and come out with some kind of insult. But the bag stayed where it was.

'There's a party next week, everyone's invited... do you want to come?'

'Whose party is it?'

'Breezy's. It's his birthday party. Hasn't he told you?'

'No, but I'd love to come,' said Jasmine, trying not to sound too excited. 'Shouldn't Breezy be inviting me, though?'

'I'm inviting you. Breezy won't mind. Everyone's coming. It's an open invite.'

Jasmine couldn't help feeling as if maybe at last things were changing and she was being accepted.

She couldn't wait to tell Devlin that afternoon. As usual he was waiting as she got off the bus at the Soup Bowl. It had become a routine since their run-in with Ronnie and his gang. Devlin was the only friend she had, and his presence at the bus stop always made her feel safe.

'Hi, Jazzie,' he smiled when he saw her. He was the first person to use her nickname in Barbados and it made her feel happy when he said it.

'I've been invited to a birthday party on Saturday night,' she blurted out.

'Hey, that's cool,' said Devlin with a slight touch of envy in his voice.

'It'll be the first time I've been out since I got here,' continued Jasmine, without noticing.

'Well, maybe you will make some new friends....'

'I hope so,' said Jasmine, looking down at the sand as she walked.

Just then the sound of hyena-like laughter split the air. Ahead of them, where the road rose up to a ridge above the beach skirting Bathsheba's small park, stood Ronnie and his gang. This time he had more cronies with him. They were looking down at Jasmine and Devlin from their vantage point, hurling abuse at them.

'Here comes Fish Boy and his English girlfriend,' they hooted.

Jasmine stopped in her tracks, frozen with fear and anxiety. 'Let's go back,' she said, her voice trembling.

Devlin glanced over his shoulder. The only other way to Grannie Braithwaites's house was by the top road and that was a long way round. And anyway, he was not going to let Ronnie and his moronic friends intimidate him. He might be outnumbered, but he knew Ronnie was a coward and would not dare to get physical, though that didn't stop the taunts and cruel words, and they hurt just as much.

'Come on,' said Devlin determinedly. 'Keep smiling as we walk past, that drives them nuts.'

Jasmine forced a smile on to her face and even managed a laugh as they drew close to their tormentors.

'Hey, Fish Boy,' jeered Ronnie. 'Going to catch my dinner?'

The other boys hooted with encouraging laughter.

'English Girl, my dad's gonna buy your house and flatten it, so you'd better start looking for somewhere to live. Perhaps you should go back home.'

'Keep smiling,' whispered Devlin as they walked past.

It seemed to be working because Ronnie was almost jumping up and down with frustration that his jibes were not getting a reaction.

'See what I mean?' grinned Devlin. 'It drives

him nuts.'

'Going home to Mummy, Fish Boy?' yelled Ronnie, almost apoplectic with rage. 'Oh, I forgot, she dead, isn't she!'

Jasmine flinched at the words. How low could this bully sink?

The smile on Devlin's face froze, and his eyes blinked as if trying to close out what he had just heard.

Ronnie stood on the ridge staring down, but his sidekicks edged away, their laughter failing them.

Ronnie nervously looked round at them for support but they shuffled uncomfortably. Ronnie's face twitched with uncertainty. He realised he had gone too far, but he stood his ground.

Jasmine looked at Devlin, and what she saw terrified her. His face was contorted into a snarl and his hands clenched and unclenched at his side. Before she could speak, Devlin was clawing his way like a demented mountain goat up the sandy face of the small cliff which separated him from Ronnie.

'No, Devlin!' she yelled.

Devlin seemed oblivious to her cries as he furiously tried to get at Ronnie.

Although the sand was soft and fell away as he

attacked it, he was making good progress towards his tormentor. He had almost reached the top when Ronnie's nerve finally broke and, with a half-hearted laugh, which sounded more like a sob, he turned and ran headlong up the hill without turning round.

'He's gone,' shouted Jasmine at the top of her voice. 'Stop, Devlin.... Stop, he's gone!'

This time Devlin reacted to the sound of her voice and stopped scrabbling at the loose sand. His body went limp as he let himself slide slowly back down the steep slope.

Jasmine ran over to where he lay on his back, breathing heavily from his exertions. Tears burst from her eyes and she dropped to her knees beside him. 'I hate this place,' she sobbed.

Devlin pushed himself up on to one elbow. 'I'm sorry,' he said. 'I lost it, didn't I?'

'But what he said was unforgivable, Devlin. You looked as though you would have have killed him if you'd reached him.'

'Yeah, he would have deserved it!'

'I'm glad you didn't. You would have been in deep trouble if you had.'

'I know,' said Devlin, looking at the blood trickling from the cuts on his hands, caused by the sharp stones in the sand. 'Come on. Grannie Braithwaite will be wondering where you are, and I've got to stop off at the store and get something for my dad.'

'What?' asked Jasmine.

'I always get him a newspaper and our weekly lotto ticket.'

They walked slowly up the hill, and Devlin gave a small wave to Grannie Braithwaite as she appeared on her veranda. 'See you tomorrow,' he said.

'Yes,' said Jasmine. 'And don't let what Ronnie did get to you. He's scum.'

Devlin nodded, before turning and trotting off towards the store. After twenty steps or so, he turned and took his customary look over his shoulder. As usual Jasmine was still there, watching him go.

Chapter Seventeen

Devlin's home was an unkempt, wooden house on one floor, with three small rooms and a tiny kitchen. It had always been spotless when his mother was alive but now it was a mess, as there was so little time to clear up.

'As long as everything is clean, that's all we need,' his dad would say in his matter-of-fact way, as he sat in his favourite chair.

Devlin changed out of his school uniform into jeans and a T-shirt, and went down to the beach where *Freedom* was moored.

'Devlin boy.... Where have you been?' Luther was struggling with a net, which looked like a tangled mess of green string. 'I need a hand with this, and there's a split in the fuel line that has to be fixed before we can go out in the morning. You haven't answered me, boy, where de heck have you been? Not with that Braithwaite girl again, I hope. She's trouble.'

Devlin still didn't say anything. He knew it wasn't

worth arguing with his dad. He just handed over the newspaper and the lotto ticket, sat down and silently started work on the net, keeping his thoughts to himself.

He wished he could talk things over with his dad, man to man. But there was no chance of that. Dad didn't do touchy-feely, and anyway, he still saw Devlin as a little boy. Jasmine was the first person, other than his mum, he had shown his emotions to, and it felt good.

The next morning the sea was calmer than it had been for the last few weeks, and the fish were swimming in plentiful shoals. Luther shouted orders as he steered the boat towards the teeming fish, which scattered in all directions, like silver arrows skimming across the water. The early morning sun created glistening showers of spray as *Freedom's* bow plunged into the waves.

'Now, Devlin boy, hoist the net in. That's all it'll take.'

Devlin hoisted in ten net-loads of silver flying fish until there was no more room in the hold.

Luther looked wistfully over his shoulder at the glittering surface of the sea, which he knew held more fish than his small boat could take. Reluctantly he gunned the engine and turned *Freedom* for home. 'Good day's work,' he said to Devlin, as he rested back in his seat.

Devlin nodded. He knew nothing made his dad happier than a successful catch.

'If we had a bigger boat, we could have pulled in ten, maybe twelve thousand fish.'

Devlin nodded again. This was another of Dad's favourite topics.

Freedom was an old boat and took a lot of maintaining. Some fishermen had new and much bigger boats, which were able to go further out and carry more fish. But they cost more money than Luther could possibly afford. So things carried on the way they were.

Devlin had been helping his father since he was eight years old. Luther never discussed the arrangement with him – he just took it for granted that Devlin would do for him what he had done for his father. Father to son – fishermen.

Devlin didn't really relish the thought of continuing the family tradition, but that was the way it was. He had no choice, it was a given. He had grown up fast since the death of his mother, and because of that he was an outsider. He didn't have any real friends, he was too busy with the boat. And when he wasn't helping with that he was studying hard to keep up with his classmates.

It was becoming harder and harder to balance school and fishing, and his schoolwork was beginning to suffer. In his heart he knew his future wasn't as a fisherman. But if he dared tell his father there would be trouble. And as if that wasn't enough, at school he was constantly called 'Fish Boy', because most of the other children's parents were professional business people.

❖ ❖ ❖

Jasmine had spent all of Saturday getting ready for the party. She had to admit she was excited, even though she knew most of the people there wouldn't talk to her. But she hoped that maybe, in a different setting, they would be friendlier.

Mum had straightened her hair and she wore one of her favourite dresses. She felt really good when she saw herself in the mirror.

Dad looked her up and down sternly when she walked into the living room, but Mum gave a reassuring smile.

'She's been getting ready all day, haven't you, Jazzie?'

Dad was still looking her up and down, and finally his eyes stopped at her knees. 'That dress is too short,' he said angrily. 'You're a twelve-year-old girl.'

'Oh Daaad, I'm nearly thirteen,' wailed Jasmine, 'and it's not short. Everyone wears skirts this short.'

'Everyone? Who's everyone? I don't care what everyone does. You're my daughter and you're not going out like that.'

'How about the blue-and-yellow dress I bought for you. That's a bit longer, isn't it?' Mum said quickly.

Jasmine knew that arguing was no use when Dad had that look on his face. She stomped out and marched angrily to her room, followed closely by Mum.

'You'll look lovely in this one,' said Mum, pulling out the blue-and-yellow dress and trying to be positive. 'It's longer.'

'It's almost down to the ground!' moaned Jasmine

'Well, it's all we've got, so I suggest you put it on. We're already late and Dad isn't going to change his mind on this, Jazzie.'

Jasmine reluctantly changed into the long, yellow-

and-blue dress which Mum had bought her when she was singing in the school Christmas concert a year before.

'Happy now?' said Jasmine, scowling at her dad.

He looked up from his paper and stared at her. Finally his face broke into a smile. 'Yes, I'm happy now. You look so pretty, sweetheart, like a princess. Have a good time... and no alcohol.'

'Yes, Dad.'

'And you know what I told you about boys.'

'Yes, Dad.'

It was about 8.30 pm when they finally got into Mum's car and set off for the party. It was a ten minute drive away and Suzanne had said to be there between seven-thirty and eight - so they were a bit late.

Mum seemed excited too, as she drove along the narrow road towards Breezy's house. 'I'll pick you up at about eleven. You've got your phone so you can call if the party ends earlier.'

'It won't, Mum, it's Saturday night.... Bye.'

The party was in a large, two-storey house set back from the road. Breezy's dad was a chef at one of the big hotels and had laid on a big spread of delicious snacks.

Most people had arrived and were in the garden,

standing round the swimming pool in groups, sipping fruit punch, talking and laughing loudly.

Jasmine nervously walked through the open gate and up the path towards the pool. Before she had gone a few steps, Maxine spotted her. She made a bee-line for her.

'Who invited you?' she yelled.

Everyone stopped talking and looked over at Jasmine.

Jasmine stopped and stared at Maxine. 'Suzanne,' she stuttered, nodding towards Suzanne, who was standing behind Maxine.

'Well, it's not her party, so she shouldn't have invited you. Should you, Suzanne?'

Suzanne just stood there hesitantly, looking round at the faces of her friends.

'It's Breezy's party and he didn't invite you, so you aren't welcome here. We don't want you, do we?' sneered Maxine, looking round at the group of partygoers.

Everyone shuffled and looked uncomfortable.

Just then Breezy came out of the house, laughing and carrying a drink. 'What's goin' on?' he grinned.

'We've got a gate-crasher, Breezy. But she's just leavin', aren't you?'

Breezy was an easy-going boy, and Maxine could twist him round her finger. She gave him one of her looks.

'I don't mind if she stays,' he said, looking for support, trying to gauge what the others were thinking.

'You didn't invite her. No one likes her. She's not one of us! Look at that stupid dress she's got on. She looks like she's wearing a Bajan flag,' scoffed Maxine, changing tack to get support. And it worked. Everyone laughed.

Jasmine felt her knees trembling and her eyes filling with tears. She hadn't thought about the colour of the dress. She felt like ripping the blue-and-yellow monstrosity off. Why hadn't Dad just let her wear the red one? She had never felt such humiliation in all her life.

Suzanne stepped forward, 'You can stay, Jasmine. Come and get a drink.'

Maxine turned on her with venom. 'Oh, so you've got a new best friend, have you, Suzanne? I hope you two are very happy together, because you and I are finished if she stays.'

Suzanne looked shocked. She had been the one Maxine had picked on until Jasmine had arrived.

Now Maxine had allowed her into her gang, as long as she did what she was told. 'I just thought it would be OK for her to come....' said Suzanne.

'Well, you were wrong. She's not welcome.'

Jasmine had had enough of this. 'Don't worry, I'm not staying. I don't want to come to a party with you lot. You all make me sick.'

She spun round and ran headlong up the path almost tripping and falling into the pool as she fumbled in her handbag for her phone as she went. 'Mum... Mum, come and get me...' she sobbed into the phone.

Within five minutes the car came slowly up the road and stopped in front of Jasmine, who was now half-running to meet it.

'What happened?' said Mum anxiously.

'I don't want to talk about it,' snapped Jasmine. 'I shouldn't have worn this stupid dress. Everyone laughed at me. It's the same at school.'

'Are you being bullied at school, Jazzie?'

Jasmine couldn't hold out any longer. 'I can't take any more, Mum,' she sobbed.

'Oh, darlin', why didn't you tell me you were being bullied?'

'You and Dad are always busy. I just thought you

wouldn't want to hear about it, you've got enough on your plates as it is,' sobbed Jasmine.

'How could you think that?' said her mum, hugging her close. 'You are the most important thing in the world to us. First thing on Monday morning I'm going to the school to speak to the Principal.'

When they got home and Dad heard what had happened, he was furious. 'What kind of school allows this to go on?' he said angrily. 'I'm coming with you on Monday. I'll give them a piece of my mind.'

❖ ❖ ❖

All three of them sat in silence outside the Principal's office. Mum had phoned at eight o'clock on the dot that morning to make the appointment, and she wasn't going to take no for an answer.

Finally, after keeping them waiting for about half an hour, the Principal's secretary said, 'Dr Mortimer will see you now.'

'What kind of school is this?' said Dad as soon as he entered the room. 'I bring my child here to Barbados to get away from nasty, vicious people, and to get a good education. I thought that's what we would find at this school.'

'Just one moment, Mr Braithwaite. Can your daughter please tell me exactly what's been going on?'

Jasmine felt a little stupid having to say no one liked her. It sounded so pathetic in her head and at that moment she couldn't bring out the words.

'Go on, Jasmine,' encouraged her mum. 'Tell Dr Mort –'

'No one makes me feel welcome here,' she whispered, 'and ...'

'More than that,' interrupted Dad. 'My daughter has had to face outright bullying since she arrived here at this school.'

'I'm sorry to hear this, Mr and Mrs Braithwaite. Whittington school prides itself on its pastoral care and takes these matters very seriously. At this school we play the role of educator, social instructor and part-time parent.'

'That may well be, but what about the bullying our daughter has had to endure over the last few months?'

'Well, if Jasmine had cared to let someone at the school know, then our guidance councillor would have given advice to her and the offending pupils. Bullying is certainly not tolerated. Perhaps, to try and integrate better, Jasmine might like take up one of the many activities offered to our pupils after school. Like tennis or drama.'

The thought of spending extra time at school with Maxine and her crowd brought dread to Jasmine's heart. But she nodded. She didn't want to look as though she was not prepared to make an effort to mix.

'But what are you going to do to the children who've been bullying Jasmine?' demanded Dad.

'I can assure you there will be repercussions, Mr Briathwaite. Leave it to me. But I need to know the names.'

Jasmine wanted to shout out Maxine at the top of her voice, but something stopped her. The word stuck in her throat.... 'No one in particular,' she mumbled.

'Tell him who it is, Jazzie,' pleaded mum.

Jasmine bowed her head and held back the tears. It was clear that she wasn't going to mention any names.

'Very well, I will speak to the whole school,' said Dr Mortimer, standing up. He was clearly very angry.

❖ ❖ ❖

The next morning, Dr Mortimer stood on the platform, staring sternly down at the assembly with a look of disappointment on his face. Everyone knew something serious was about to happen and there was a feeling of trepidation in the hall.

'There are those amongst us,' his booming voice echoed off the walls, 'who have not considered the reputation of this great school and have abused their privileges. Our code of honour is to 'Serve one another in Comradeship'. That has been so since the school's beginnings. But, I am saddened to say, it has been brought to my attention that this code has been broken. Some of our pupils have been made to feel unwelcome and not part of our fraternity. This must stop immediately. I want every pupil to practise our code. I personally will be keeping an eye on everyone. I will be watching you!'

Jasmine didn't dare to look at anyone in the hushed hall, but she could feel Maxine's penetrating eyes on her back. She was beginning to wonder if she should have kept her mouth shut.

Chapter Eighteen

Luther was worried. *Freedom* was taking on water, and the knowledge that he would be unable to fish while she was being repaired drove him to put in as many hours fishing as he could.

He usually went out either in the early morning or late afternoon, and got back before sunset. But now he was doing both the morning and evening trips, and staying out later too. Sometimes he and Devlin didn't get back until well after sundown, and it was only due to Luther's skill and experience that they managed to navigate their way home safely.

One evening they were fishing not far off-shore. The sea was calm and the fish were plentiful. They could see the twinkling lights of Bathsheba in the distance, but the darkness was rapidly closing around them like a velvet blanket. *Freedom* bobbed on the light swell, her engine silent, the only sound coming from the waves slapping against her flanks. Devlin had to admit that on nights like this, the beauty and serenity of the sea was a magical experience.

'OK,' announced Luther, 'we'd better call it a day, Devlin boy. Haul in that net. It's getting too dark to see now anyway. Time to put our lights on and head back.'

Devlin was relieved that at last they were going home. He had geography homework to finish and it was almost nine o'clock.

Luther was just about to start the engine and turn on *Freedom's* running lights when out of the darkness came a noise. It was a low, rumbling throb which vibrated in the air. It seemed to surround the tiny fishing boat, growing louder and closer with every passing second.

Luther scrabbled for the flashlight he kept stowed in a wooden box next to the wheel, but before he could find it the noise was almost on top of them.

Devlin stood frozen in the bow of *Freedom* as a long, low, sinister shape slid past only metres away from where he stood. It was about fifty feet long, from its thin, sharply pointed bow to its stern, on which sat two massive outboard engines.

The speedboat was painted grey from stem to stern and not a single running light shone to alert other vessels of her presence.

'What de heck!' exclaimed Luther.

Devlin stared at the back of the awe-inspiring machine as it disappeared, its propellers leaving a trail of white foam. He could just make out the word *Barracuda* painted in silver on her rear.

'You crazy maniac!' Luther yelled at the top of his voice. But whoever was at the wheel was oblivious to them, and could not hear over the throb of its engines. 'People like that shouldn't be allowed on the water,' muttered Luther, starting up *Freedom's* engine. 'Let's get back home before he comes back for a second try at us.'

As Luther steered *Freedom* close to the shore using landmarks to guide him, Devlin spotted the dark shape of the *Barracuda* again, faintly illuminated by the lights of a pick-up truck parked on the beach. It was moored now, just twenty metres out from the shore, in a small inlet called Craggy Bay. A rubber dingy with two men in it was skipping across the waves towards it.

Luther didn't notice. He was too busy concentrating on getting *Freedom* safely back and unloading the catch.

❖ ❖ ❖

At school, things continued to go badly for Jasmine. Nothing was said, but now Maxine and her posse completely ignored her. Their jibes and sneering comments had stopped, but if looks could kill she would surely have been dead.

One day Maxine didn't turn up for school and Jasmine felt a sense of relief, as well as a slight hope that Maxine might be ill. She felt pleased, but guilty about hoping Maxine was really sick and suffering from some horrible illness.

At lunchtime, Breezy sidled over to where Jasmine sat in her usual refuge under a tree. 'Hey, English, what's up?'

Jasmine knew he was only talking to her openly because Maxine wasn't around. However, she was glad to have someone to talk to. 'Hi, I wish you wouldn't call me that. My name's Jasmine.'

Breezy shrugged, 'Everyone calls you English, it's your nickname. You shouldn't be so uptight about it!'

Jasmine felt the urge to tell him just how uptight she really was about the so-called stupid nickname, but she restrained herself and said instead, 'Where's Maxine today? She's never too far away from you."

'Yeah, she's off today, she's in court with her parents.'

'What have they done?' said Jasmine.

'They're getting divorced and they're fighting over who gets her.'

Jasmine was shocked by the way Breezy announced this. She had no idea that Maxine's parents were splitting up. For a moment she imagined what it would be like if her parents did the same, and shuddered at the thought. 'Wow! I never knew about that,' she said.

'Everybody knows about it, it was a big scandal last year,' shrugged Breezy. 'Her dad had a ting with a woman – she was like you.'

Jasmine was shocked. 'What do you mean, like me?' she demanded.

'Y'know, a Bajan who grew up in England and came back to live here, an English. Now he's shacked up with her and he wants Maxine to live with him and his English woman. Maxine hates her. She says English come back here, showing off with lots of money and fancy ideas, which took her dad away.'

Jasmine listened intently.

'Now her mum's mash up....'

'Mash up?' quizzed Jasmine.

'Yes, mash up! A wreck. She don't go out much and she's hitting the bottle. That's why Maxine's dad wants to get her away from her. So they're in court arguing about custard.'

'Custody!' corrected Jasmine.

'Yeah, that's what I meant... custard. Anyway, I gotta go now,' said Breezy. 'Nice talking to ya...'

Jasmine waved to him as he strutted off in his usual way. She leant back against her tree and thought about what Breezy had just said. And gradually it dawned on her. Perhaps Maxine hated her because she despised anyone who reminded her of the English woman who had taken away her dad and broken up her family... Not that knowing this made Jasmine feel any less miserable....

The bell rang to mark the end of break. She gathered up her bag and headed slowly back into class ready for another round of torment.

Chapter Nineteen

It was a big relief for Jasmine when the Christmas holidays finally arrived.

Mum and Dad had arranged for her to stay with Grannie Braithwaite for the first week, so that she wouldn't be at home alone when they were busy at work.

Jasmine was glad about this. She adored the beauty of Bathsheba and the gentle love of her grannie.

Christmas was rapidly approaching and for Jasmine it was bizarre to hear *I'm dreaming of a white Christmas* being played on the radio and seeing snowmen and reindeer displayed in shop windows in the shopping mall, while outside the sun beamed down, as always.

It was traditional for all families to make moist, rich Christmas cake, full of fruit and rum as well as cooking succulent Bajan ham, flavoured with sugar, pineapple and cloves.

Grannie Braithwaite was busy getting ready to

cook hers, and she encouraged Jasmine to help her with the preparations. 'This is a family recipe that I'm passing down to you, my darlin',' she smiled. 'One day you will be cooking this for your children.'

Jasmine spent the whole day helping Grannie Braithwaite to mix the cake and put the final touches to the ham, ready for the oven. It was tiring work but the delicious, mouthwatering smells made the experience a joyful one.

Finally Grannie Braithwaite sat down with a loud sigh. 'Well, girl, we've finished and I'm exhausted. I think I'll sit down for a while.'

Jasmine was tired too, but she offered to make a drink for Grannie Braithwaite.

'Thank you, darlin', that's just what I needed. What's that beeping noise?'

'Oh, it's my phone. Devlin just sent me a text. He wants to meet up at the beach. I won't be long, Grannie. Is that all right?' said Jasmine.

'OK, darlin', don't be too long though. It's nearly dark and there aren't many lights out there on the roads.'

Devlin was waiting in the usual place and looked excited to see Jasmine. 'Hi, Jazzie, how's it going?'

'Great. What have you been up to?'

'Oh, the usual, working for my dad.'

'It's not much holiday fun for you, is it?'

'My dad don't do holidays,' shrugged Devlin. 'What are you doing tomorrow morning?'

'Nothin' much.'

'There's something I want to show you. Can you meet me about ten? My dad will have unloaded the catch and when we're done I can meet you.'

'OK. Where are we going?' asked Jasmine.

'Wait and see,' said Devlin mysteriously.

It was a beautiful evening and they decided to take a walk to the other end of Bathsheba, away from the cluster of houses where Grannie Braithwaite lived. The streets were quiet, but Jasmine felt no sense of danger as they walked past the row of wooden houses which faced the beach.

The moonless sky shimmered with millions of stars, more than Jasmine could ever have imagined to exist, back in London. The roar of the sea was accompanied by a glorious symphony of crickets and frogs making their night music.

The road angled slightly left and climbed steeply. On the bend was a cafe which was frequented by surfers and a few tourists. Jasmine and Devlin looked through the window as they walked past. A crowd of young people stood around the bar laughing and talking loudly. Jasmine wondered what it would be like to rule your own life and not always be told what to do.

'Come on, let's get back,' said Devlin, snapping her back to reality.

They turned and walked back toward Grannie Braithwaite's house. Ahead of them the deserted road was lit by a single street lamp, its dim orange glow casting a small circle of light on to the tarmac.

Suddenly Jasmine and Devlin tensed as three men stepped into the circle of light. They were dressed in dark trousers and black leather jackets. Two of them looked tall and well-built, and were aged about thirty. The third one stood with his back to them so Jasmine and Devlin couldn't see his face. But Jasmine thought there was something vaguely familiar about the way he stood. His leather jacket stretched tightly across his enormous, muscular shoulders.

As they watched, the man's phone must have vibrated on silent, because he fumbled inside his jacket to answer it. He turned, and as the light caught his face Jasmine jumped with surprise.

'Look, Devlin, it's Chief Inspector Alleyne. What's he doing over this side of the island?'

Instinctively Jasmine and Devlin pulled further back into the shadows between two buildings.

'Hello, yeah... we're about to get in position, so stand by. If they try to land the stuff tonight we'll be waiting for them. Yeah, OK, bye.' He flipped his phone closed and put it back in his pocket. 'OK, let's go,' he said, walking quickly towards the craggy shoreline.

Jasmine and Devlin emerged from their hiding place, hearts beating fast. This was scary, but exciting at the same time.

Jasmine knew she should be heading back to Grannie Braithwaite's, but curiosity was swiftly getting the better of her. 'Let's follow them,' she whispered.

Devlin nodded. He too was intrigued.

Keeping low and in the shadows, they quickly headed after the three men. They were rapidly disappearing into the encroaching darkness, along a rock-strewn pathway which led between thorny bushes and massive boulders.

It was so dark that Jasmine and Devlin almost stumbled into the men, who had stopped behind a big rock. They were looking intently out to sea. Devlin pulled Jasmine down behind a bush.

'What are they up to?' asked Jasmine, as Devlin

strained to see what the men were looking at. But there was only the dark void of sky and the darker sea, flecked by the occasional white-topped waves.

The only sound that could be heard was the distant, relentless roaring of the breakers, and the low hiss of the wind. Minutes ticked by as they waited expectantly for something to happen.

Jasmine's bent knees started to cramp. Slowly she tried to change her position without making a noise. But she hadn't realised that right behind her was a large aloe plant and, as she shifted, one of its sharp, spiny leaves jabbed itself into her backside. She let out a loud yelp of shock mixed with pain.

Chief Inspector Alleyne spun round, his powerful torch catching Jasmine and Devlin in its beam like frightened rabbits. 'What the heck are you two doing here?' he exploded.

Jasmine and Devlin stood petrified, shielding their eyes.

'OK, boys, I know these two. I think we had better call it a night. No one's likely to turn up now.'

The other two men looked at Jasmine and Devlin with a mixture of annoyance and curiosity. Jasmine noticed that when they moved, their jackets opened to reveal what looked like small sub-machine guns tucked into their belts.

Chief Inspector Alleyne was on his phone again. 'Yeah, nothing tonight, we'll try again tomorrow,' he said, snapping his phone shut.

'What were you looking for, Inspector Alleyne?' asked Jasmine innocently.

'Chief Inspector!' said the big policeman. 'Look, little girl, you seem to have a way of causing trouble. Do you realise you two could have endangered my whole operation, sneaking around in the bushes like that? I thought I told you to stay out of trouble. And as for you, young man, you should know better. I thought you were a smart kid.'

Jasmine and Devlin just stood still, looking sheepishly at him.

He turned to his two men. 'Give us a minute, boys.' He jerked his head towards the road and they sauntered away. 'Listen, you two, I want you to keep this to yourselves. If anyone finds out we were waiting here it could wreck everything. We got a lead that a boat comes in loaded with drugs every week. We were waiting to intercept it and watch where the drugs are taken. Trouble is, we don't know where and when, so we are trying to watch out for any suspicious activity along this coast. Do you understand?'

Jasmine nodded.

'I know where the boat comes in,' said Devlin in a matter-of-fact voice. 'I even know the name of it. My dad and I saw it a while back when we were out fishing late one night. It nearly sliced my dad's boat in half.'

Chief Inspector Alleyne stared at Devlin intently. 'Good Lord, boy, this is fantastic. Tell me all about it.'

Devlin related the whole story about the *Barracuda* and its rendezvous in Craggy Bay.

When he had finished, Chief Inspector Alleyne looked triumphant. 'This is the break we've been waiting for. Please keep this meeting to yourselves, you two. No one must know. Now it's late - shouldn't you be getting home?'

Jasmine and Devlin ran all the way back to Grannie Braithwaite's, brimming with excitement after they had vowed to keep the secret.

'See you tomorrow,' said Devin, as he jogged away. When he reached the first street light he turned back and gave a wave, before turning right on to the beach and disappearing into the darkness.

That night, as Jasmine slept, her dreams were full of James Bond adventures.

❖ ❖ ❖

Dave arrived early for work on Monday morning. O'Brien had given him an ultimatum: either get back on schedule with the work or lose the contract. So he was keen to get going.

Usually the guys were gathered in a downstairs room in the development, which was eventually going to be the reception area. But at the moment it was being used to store the gear and materials for the workmen who were fitting all the bathrooms and kitchens.

Dave was surprised to find no one there except old Jed. He was one of the carpenters, and he tended to get on with his work quietly and keep himself to himself.

'Where is everybody, Jed?' said Dave anxiously, looking at his watch.

'Vince has taken them for a coffee in the cafe up the road,' replied Jed, looking over the top of his newspaper. 'I prefer to stay here, though. I don't like coffee.'

'Why on earth did Vince do that?' said Dave incredulously. 'He's never done it before.'

'Search me,' shrugged Jed.

'Well, you get started and I'll go and get them back here. It's gone eight and we're well behind.'

'OK, boss, I'll just finish my paper then I'll get started.'

'Now!' snapped Dave. 'You can read your paper in your own time.'

He found Vince and the other six guys sitting at a table outside the cafe. He marched up and tapped his watch. 'Any chance of you lot starting work?' he demanded.

Vince, who had elected himself as a sort of unofficial foreman, looked up. 'Hey, boss, keep cool, we just havin' our mornin' coffee.'

'Morning coffee! Since when do you have morning coffee? You've never done it before.'

'Well, we heard it's an English tradition, you know, tea break and all that.'

The rest of the guys laughed loudly.

'Look, you lot. I don't know what you're playing at, but we are well behind. Mr O'Brien is coming today to see what progress has been made since last week, and you lot are sitting around drinking coffee.'

'OK, boss,' said Vince, 'we'll get straight on it, right, guys?' The other men nodded half-heartedly. 'You guys get back, I'll pay for the coffee.'

They slowly got up and sauntered back up the road toward the site.

Dave waited for Vince, who pulled a crisp, twenty-dollar note from his wallet and left it on the table.

'You're in a generous mood today,' said Dave.

'Well, I backed the right horse at races at the Garrison at the weekend.'

The Garrison Savannah was where everyone in Barbados went to watch horse racing and bet on the horses, which were owned by people like O'Brien and Harrison.

'Look, Vince, we've got to work faster. The job's getting behind and O'Brien's breathing down my neck. See what you can do with the guys, can't you?'

Vince looked at Dave sideways. 'You askin' me to help you? You come here from England and think you can just take over and get all the work? Listen, it's your problem not mine. If you can't handle it you shouldn't have come here. This is how we work in Barbados, at our own speed. Don't worry, the work will get done... eventually.'

He swaggered away, up the muddy road towards the site, leaving Dave standing speechless.

He couldn't understand why Vince was being so difficult.

At the beginning of the job he and all the other guys had seemed so grateful for the work and keen to get on with it. But in the last month they had become surly and their work rate had slowed to almost a standstill.

Later that day O'Brien turned up at the site and was not impressed. 'Look, Dave, I stuck my neck out for you because you told me you could do this job on time and on budget. But you're weeks behind. This is your last chance. If you don't get back on target, I'm going to start deducting penalty payments. It's all there in the contract. I'm entitled to hold back payment if the job isn't done by the 28th of February next year. That's two months away.'

Dave dejectedly watched O'Brien drive away. It was all going wrong, his Bajan dream was unravelling and there was nothing he could do about it.

His thoughts were interrupted by the ring of his mobile. It was Carlton Harrison.

'Dave, how's it going? I hear you're having a few problems. Maybe it's time you had a re-think about my proposition.'

'Get lost, Harrison!' snapped Dave. 'I told you before, Summerland House isn't for sale so you can save on your phone bill by not calling me again.'

With that, Dave snapped his phone shut and walked purposefully towards the building site.

He'd been through many challenges and adversities in his life and he wasn't about to let this one beat him, even if he had to fit all the kitchens himself.

Chapter Twenty

The morning was clear and bright, with a soft breeze blowing off the sea, as Jasmine made her way down to the beach.

Devlin was waiting for her. He was gazing out towards the sea, casually throwing small stones, which plopped noiselessly into the waves.

'Hi, Dev,' said Jasmine softly, not wishing to startle him.

'Jazzie!' he half sang as he jumped to his feet.

'You looked far away. What were you thinking about?'

'Nothin' much.' He shrugged.

'Yes, you were. You were miles away. Tell me.'

It was not in Devlin's nature to divulge his innermost thoughts to anyone, and he struggled to find an appropriately flippant response to Jasmine's request. But after a second or two he gave up. 'I was thinking about my mother,' he said, tossing his last stone into the sea. 'Come on. I hope you like walking. It's this way.'

Jasmine followed him up the hill. 'Do you still miss her?'

'It's not something you get over.'

Jasmine thought about her own parents and how she sometimes despised them. But the thought of one of them dying made her tremble with fear. And she realised at that moment, deep down, how much she loved them.

Devlin led her down a path which forked away from the road and into an area of sugar cane and dense undergrowth, where majestic mahogany trees towered over them.

Suddenly Devlin put his hand on her shoulder and placed his finger to his lips. He pointed up into the canopy of trees. At first Jasmine couldn't understand what he was pointing at, but then she saw a movement in the branches. A small green face looked down at her with two bright eyes.

'Oh my God, it's a monkey!' exclaimed Jasmine.

At this the monkey shrieked and jumped noisily to a nearby branch. In a flash the branches came alive with six or seven other monkeys, which had been so well camouflaged that Jasmine had not seen them until they moved. Two or three of them were carrying tiny babies, which clung on to their mothers tightly.

'I didn't know there were monkeys in Barbados!' Jasmine laughed with delight.

Devlin nodded. 'Yep, but the farmers hate them, they eat all the mangoes.'

They continued to walk through the overgrown bushes and trees. Jasmine was glad she had worn her jeans and not her shorts, as the thorns pulled mercilessly at her legs.

By now the sun was high in the sky and even with the shade of the trees it was becoming uncomfortably hot. After a while they passed a crumbling wall which surrounded a great plantation house.

'That's Boddrington Hall, and all these fields belong to it,' said Devlin, pushing aside some dense undergrowth.

He turned into a steep gully, which led into a flat clearing surrounded by trees. 'Here it is,' he said triumphantly. pointing to what looked like a pile of old moss-covered stones, half buried in ferns and vines.

'You brought me all this way to see a pile of stones?' exclaimed Jasmine, planting her hands on her hips.

'It's not a pile of stones. Look.'

Devlin roughly pulled away handfuls of thick ivy and ferns, sending birds squawking noisily into the air. After a minute or two he had cleared enough for Jasmine to see it was a long, low building about seven or eight metres long and five wide. At one end was an opening with rough stone steps leading down into a dark doorway.

'What on earth is it?' she whispered in the strange silence that seemed to have fallen on the clearing.

'It's part of the old slave quarters,' Devlin said, with reverence in his voice. 'Come and have a look.' He beckoned as he stepped gingerly down the stairs.

Jasmine followed him carefully into the dank, musty gloom. Most of the roof had rotted away, replaced by a latticework of branches through which shafts of sunlight flickered.

As her eyes grew accustomed to the semi-darkness, Jasmine looked around. The floor was made of heavy flagstones and the walls were built solidly from great blocks of the same stone.

'It's where they kept the new slaves,' said Devlin. 'Here's where they were chained.' He pointed to a thick, rusting, iron ring attached to the wall.

Jasmine tried to imagine what it must have been like all those centuries ago to be chained, beaten and abused. She had done a project about slavery at school back in London, during Black History Month. She'd cried when she had heard how the enslaved Africans suffered. Now she was standing in this dark, dank dungeon, where some of those atrocities against humanity had taken place.

Suddenly the room started to come alive. Jasmine became aware of an intense, overwhelming feeling she had never experienced before. It crept up her spine and held her chest like a vice, restricting her breathing so that her lungs struggled for air. Her ears hummed and popped as a rhythmic pounding grew inside her head.

The shafts of light seemed to dance crazily across the floor and suddenly the drumming was joined by voices. At first humming, then chanting strange words, which she somehow knew were from a far-distant continent and had their roots in her innermost ancestral memory. They swirled into her consciousness from the darkest corners of the room, gradually rising into a crescendo of African heartbeat.

But then there was a subtle change, and she thought she could hear screams and moans and the rattling of chains, which rose above the heartbeat, drowning it out in a cacophony of horror.

Jasmine put her hands to the side of her head and her body began to sway uncontrollably. She felt as though she was being overpowered by a ghostly spirit that was taking over her soul. The noise grew louder and louder and she let out a piercing scream in an unearthly voice.

Suddenly her knees began to weaken and her breathing came in short gasps. The room started to revolve slowly around her, gradually increasing in speed. She was just about to crumple to the floor when Devlin's strong hands held her elbows and pushed her up the stone steps into the sunlight above.

She took several faltering steps and then dropped to her knees, sobbing softly, like someone who has just awakened from a nightmare.

'What's the matter? What is it?' Devlin asked anxiously. 'Are you ill?'

'I heard them! I heard the slaves... I heard them screaming... it was horrible!'

Devlin looked confused. He was a practical soul, not very good at understanding deep, spiritual emotions. His serious face contorted with the effort of finding the right thing to say.

'I'm sorry I brought you here,' he said finally.

'I didn't realise it would upset you so much. I used to come here and play when I was young. My mother said it was a place that was steeped in our history.'

'I'm all right, Devlin,' said Jasmine, trying to get control of herself. 'It's all right… it's not your fault, you don't have to be sorry.'

'It was strange, seeing you like that.'

'I know, but it was a very spiritual place. I just got a bit carried away, that's all. It was the thought of all those people, taken away from their homeland and chained in that dark place. Made to be somewhere they didn't want to be. I can understand how they must have felt, cos I feel like those people who were chained up in there. I've been brought here against my will and I hate it here. My parents don't understand or care.'

'I wish I could make you feel happy, Jazzie,' said Devlin.

Jasmine laughed. 'There's only one thing that will make me happy and that's getting back to London where I belong. I'm sick of Maxine and Ronnie and all of them. They hate me just because I'm different.'

'They hate me for the same reason.'

'But at least it's your home. Mine's four thousand miles away. But I'm going back, even if I have to swim.'

Devlin stood up and walked back to the top of the stone steps. He gazed down into the darkness for a few seconds. 'There is a way, if you really want to get back. I mean a real way, not stealing a little motor boat.'

Jasmine flinched with embarrassment. 'What way?'

'Every six weeks a ship leaves for England loaded with sugar. My Uncle Norris works at the docks, and I often go there to watch them load it.'

Jasmine's eyes widened. 'Are you suggesting I stow away on it?'

Devlin shrugged. 'Can you think of a better idea?'

Jasmine's heart raced. No, she couldn't think of a better idea. Her futile attempt to escape back to England had been doomed from the beginning. But the idea of getting on board a ship sounded as if it might have a chance.

Maybe it would work.

'What will you do if you make it to England?'

'I don't know, but it will make my parents move back there.'

'But where will you stay when you get back?'

'With my friend Michaela... I've already told her I'm going to find a way to get home.'

'Well, we'll see... but I'm not promising anything though.'Devlin looked at his watch. 'It's getting late, I have to get back. My dad will be wondering where I am.... C'mon, let's go.'

When they arrived back at Grannie Braithwaite's, Jasmine's parents were waiting. Their car was packed with Grannie Braithwaite's suitcase, the precious Christmas cake sealed in a tin and the ham wrapped carefully in foil. Grannie Braithwaite was coming over to Summerland House to spend Christmas with them.

'Hi Jazzie, go and get your things. We're ready to go,' said Mum.

'Wait here,' said Jasmine to Devlin, running inside.

Dave and Marcia had not seen Devlin since the incident with the stolen boat. They had heard from Grannie Braithwaite that Jasmine had formed a friendship, so they were glad to see him.

'Hello, Devlin, did you and Jasmine have a nice day?' asked Marcia.

'Yes, Ma'am,' replied Devlin self-consciously, wishing Jasmine would hurry, so he could escape.

In her room Jasmine shoved the last few things into her bag, picked up a small parcel wrapped in Christmas paper, then ran back to where Devlin stood, uncomfortably surrounded by adults on the veranda.

'Sorry about that,' said Jasmine, pulling Devlin away by his arm.

'Bye, Devlin,' chorused Mum, Dad and Grannie Braithwaite. 'Have a good Christmas.'

'And you. Bye,' said Devlin shyly, as he followed Jasmine to the bottom of the wooden stairs.

'I bought you a Christmas present,' said Jasmine excitedly, handing Devlin the small package. Devlin looked surprised, but his face quickly changed and he stared at the ground.

'What's the matter?' asked Jasmine.

'I didn't get you anything... I'm sorry, money's tight at the moment.'

Jasmine felt stupid... she should have realised Devlin wouldn't be able to buy anything. 'It doesn't matter, Devlin. You've given me the best Christmas present I could ever have.'

Devlin looked up. 'What?' he said in confusion.

'Your friendship, silly,' smiled Jasmine.

'Oh, that...' said Devlin, the grin returning to his

face. 'No problem.'

'See you after Christmas,' said Jasmine.

'Yeah, Happy Christmas,' said Devlin awkwardly.

'Right, let's get going' interrupted Dad, looking at his watch.

Devlin turned away and walked off towards the beach. As usual, when he reached the bend he turned to see if Jasmine was still there.

As Jasmine watched him, she wished he was coming to spend Christmas with her.

'Come on, Jazzie, get in,' called Mum impatiently.

As she settled in the back of the car, Grannie Braithwaite grasped her hand happily. 'This will be the first Christmas I've spent with my family for years.'

'And it will be my first Christmas in Barbados with you, Grannie B,' said Jasmine. 'I never thought there would be much fuss about Christmas over here.'

'Oh, we know how to celebrate in style,' laughed Grannie Braithwaite, tapping the tin containing the cake.

❖ ❖ ❖

Mum and Dad had tried their hardest to make the house look Christmassy.

The tree wasn't real like the one they had back in London, but it did look lovely sitting by the open doors leading to the veranda. Of course there was no fireplace for Santa's Christmas stocking, so Mum had put it under the tree instead.

Yet Jasmine couldn't help thinking about how much she missed her friends in London. Christmas had been such an exciting time as they all discussed what presents they were going to get each other, and the presents they were going to get from their parents. This year there was none of that for Jasmine. She certainly hadn't exchanged any presents with anyone at school.

The first thing she did on Christmas morning was to text Happy Xmas to Michaela, Sam and Rachel, who she knew were already halfway through their Christmas day. She hoped they would text her back soon.

After sampling Grannie Braithwaite's delicious ham for breakfast, they gathered round the tree and opened their presents. As usual, Mum, in her practical way, had bought her mostly clothes, which Jasmine tried to sound enthusiastic about but really didn't like at all. Dad gave her a tennis racquet, as he was always going on about her becoming a tennis star. He had even been trying to persuade her to join the after-school tennis club. But Jasmine couldn't stand tennis.

After the opening of the presents they all went to church. It was decorated with red hibiscus flowers, which only blossomed at Christmas. There was much singing and praising.

Then the preacher, Reverend Rock, stood high up on the pulpit and told the nativity story in his booming voice, which caused Grannie Braithwaite and the other elderly women sporadically to shout out 'Halleluiah'. Jasmine found the whole experience strangely uplifting.

The rest of the day was spent eating, and a big fuss was made about Grannie Braithwaite's Christmas cake, which Jasmine had to admit was delicious. They watched DVDs of old films, which her mum loved, and just sat around chatting.

Frankly it wasn't much fun for Jasmine, so in the afternoon she took a quick walk down to the beach. It was crowded with tourists who had decided to leave the freezing cold in Britain for the Bajan weather. She was sure she spotted a famous pop star on the beach but thought she might be seeing things. She loved hearing the English accents. It made her feel nearer to England.

Just then her phone beeped. At last it was a text from Michaela. 'Yeah, Happy Xmas, hope u r havin fun. lol M.' it said. Nothing came back from the other two and Jasmine got the feeling they were forgetting about her already. She had to get back to England to keep their friendship alive.

Chapter Twenty-one

On Boxing Day Jasmine's mum woke up full of excitement. She had been trying on hats and dresses all week for this special Bank Holiday. The bank she worked for was the main sponsor at the Garrison Savannah's family race meeting and Marcia had been given four tickets for the day. Dave wasn't too keen on going but Marcia insisted that he should take some time off, especially as it was Christmas.

'Oh, come on, Dave, it will be fun. Horse racing's something we've never gone to before.'

'Well, all right,' said Dave reluctantly.

'Great.... Now, which dress should I wear? The green or the blue?'

As usual, Jasmine wasn't asked whether she wanted to go or not. She was told she would be going and what she would wear.

'I don't want to go to a stupid horse race,' she moaned. 'It will be full of grown-ups, I'll go mad with boredom.'

'It'll be exciting,' said her mum. 'You like horses, don't you?'

'Whatever gave you that idea?' asked Jasmine, snorting with derision.

'Well, you used to love that toy one I bought you for your birthday.'

'What, My Little Pony? I was six and it was purple with a yellow mane!'

'Anyway you're coming and that's final,' said her mum, who was really looking forward to mixing with the high-society types. She felt it was almost like going to Ascot. For Jasmine it was only the thought of having Grannie Braithwaite with them that made the idea less painful.

Dave dressed in his best suit, Marcia eventually decided on a white dress and hat, Grannie Braithwaite wore a flowery dress and straw hat, and Jasmine a horrid pink dress her mum had bought in the sale. Then they all headed off to the Garrison Savannah, near Bridgetown.

Jasmine was expecting it to be full of rich people with big hats on, but she was surprised to see just about every kind of person imaginable there. Crowds were thronging the big grandstand. Even tourists mingled with the locals, who crowded round stalls selling every type of food, from fresh coconuts to barbecued flying fish. Whole families with tiny babies and ancient grannies were there, as well as affluent politicians and big-time gamblers.

The bank had a corporate box in the grandstand overlooking the famous Paddock Bend.

'So good of you to come,' beamed Victor Stoute, the bank's director. 'You must be..?'

'Marcia Braithwaite. I work at the Sunset Crest branch. This is my husband, Dave, his mum, Veronica, and our daughter, Jasmine.'

'Have you met my wife, Geraldine?'

A tall woman wearing a huge, feathery, purple hat stepped forward, smiling falsely. Jasmine noticed that some of her red lipstick had transferred itself to her front teeth.

'So pleased to meet you,' she gushed. 'Do help yourself to drinks, and there's some food on its way up. Enjoy your day.'

Then she spotted someone else over Dave's shoulder and was gone as quickly as she had appeared, her feathered hat wafting majestically in the wind.

Jasmine looked round the room. No one seemed interested in talking to her so she went over to the balcony. Directly under the grandstand was an open area thronging with people. They pressed up against a wooden fence which separated them from a vast open area of grass. On the platform opposite stood a life-size statue of a race horse, which sparkled in the sunshine. Far in the distance, Jasmine could see a group of jockeys mounted on gleaming horses.

Suddenly a loud bell sounded and the dozen horses and riders exploded on to the course. A voice from the speakers shouted 'They're off!', and everyone surged forward. At first there was a hushed silence. Then, as the pack of horses sped towards them, the crowd erupted, each person screaming the name of the horse which was printed on the white ticket they held aloft.

The roar grew to a crescendo as the horses, their hooves pounding and their riders straining every muscle to urge them on, thundered past the stand. The leading jockey waved his hand above his head in victory.

'Wow! That was amazing!' shrieked Jasmine, jumping up and down with excitement.

'Well, I just lost five dollars,' said Dad, tearing up his white slip. 'Betting is a mug's game. I'm going to get some food.'

The next race wasn't for a while so Jasmine

decided to take a look around. She made her way to the area behind the grandstand, where crowds of people were watching the magnificent, muscular horses being saddled up. The jockeys, who were all dressed in brightly coloured outfits, strutted around like peacocks, stared at by adoring fans, who treated them like superstars.

Out of the blue Jasmine heard her name being called. 'Jasmine! Jasmine Braithwaite, hello!'

Jasmine looked around and recognised a familiar face in the crowd. It was Suzanne Thomas, who rushed over to her.

'Oh, hello,' said Jasmine coolly.

'What are you doing here?' said Suzanne as if this was the last place on earth she expected to find Jasmine.

'What are *you* doing here?' countered Jasmine.

'Oh, my dad owns one of the horses, that one over there.' She pointed to a shiny black horse with the number 4 on its side.

'How nice for you.'

'Look, Jasmine, I'm sorry about what happened at the party. It was all my fault, I shouldn't have invited you.'

'Yeah, whatever.'

'No, I'm really sorry.'

'I suppose it wasn't your fault,' admitted Jasmine. 'Maxine was the one who accused me of gate-crashing. She's evil, and one of these days she's going to get her come-uppance.'

Suzanne looked down at her feet. 'I hope so, because she picks on everyone. Before you arrived it was me. She made my life a misery.'

'Well, why doesn't somebody do something? Why can't they stand up to her?'

'I dunno, she just so clever at getting people to do what she wants.'

'She's a bully, and one day she's going to get found out.'

'Look, Jasmine, can we be friends, I mean outside school? I don't live far from you, we could hang out together.'

'You mean we don't speak to each other when Maxine's around. Is that what you're saying?'

Suzanne looked embarrassed. 'Look, I've got to go, my dad's horse is in the next race. I'll see you around.'

'Yeah, as long as Maxine isn't there.'

Suzanne disappeared into the crowd and Jasmine made her way back to the grandstand.

'Where have you been?' asked Dad, munching on a barbecued chicken leg.

'Oh, just looking around,' said Jasmine. 'Where's Mum?'

'She's been invited to go with her bank friends to hand out the prize to the owner of the winning horse. Hey, should we have a flutter on the next race?'

'I thought you said it was a mug's game?'

'Yeah, well, it is, but it adds excitement,' chuckled Dad. 'You choose a horse.'

'Number four,' answered Jasmine spontaneously.

'OK, number four it is, I'll go and stick ten dollars on it.'

'I'll stay here with Grannie B.'

Dave went down to the crowded booth, where people were pushing and shoving to get their bets on before the race. He just managed to put his on before the window closed and a bell rang to signal the race was about to start.

He pushed his way through the crowd and had just turned into the corridor leading back to the stairs when he saw something which made him freeze in his tracks.

There, in a quiet corner, away from prying eyes, stood Carlton Harrison. Hidden slightly behind a concrete pillar was another man. Dave pulled back into the shadow and watched as Harrison pulled out a wad of bank notes and carefully counted them out into the outstretched hand of the other man.

Harrison laughed loudly, slapped the man on the back and walked away, up the corridor. The other man turned and came towards where Dave was pressed against the wall. Dave almost let out a gasp as the man drew level with him. It was Vince, chuckling happily to himself as he stuffed the money into his pocket and strode into the sunlight.

Dave was stunned. Vince had never mentioned he knew Harrison, and yet here he was, getting what looked like a large amount of cash from him.

Suddenly it hit Dave like a sledgehammer. Vince was the one who was the trouble-maker at work. He was always encouraging the others to 'take it easy' or to 'do it tomorrow'. And now he was treating the other guys to coffee-breaks out of his own pocket. Dave put two and two together. Vince must be working for Harrison!

He walked back to the grandstand in a state of shock, and got back to the box just as the race was on the home straight. Jasmine was jumping up and down as the horses galloped past the stand. 'Come on, number four!' she screamed.

The horses flashed by and crossed the finish line, the ground shaking beneath their hooves. The announcer's voice blared out over the roar of the crowd. 'And horse number four, Homeward Bound, is the winner at twenty to one.'

'You see, Dad, I told you number four would win!' said Jasmine, her eyes bright with excitement. This was the first time since she had arrived in Barbados that she was actually enjoying herself.

'That's great, but we're going home now,' said Dave, his mind still reeling from his encounter in the corridor.

'Oh, Dad,' moaned Jasmine. 'Can't we choose a horse in the next race? Do we have to go?'

'Yes, we do,' said Dave. 'Anyway, they say you should quit while you're ahead. So tell Gran and your mother to meet me by the pay-out booth.'

Jasmine came back down to earth with a bang, her joyfulness crushed in an instant. The little piece of happiness she had experienced just for a moment was gone. She thought that, as usual, Dad was being unfair, and that he just didn't seem to care how she felt.

Chapter Twenty-two

After the Christmas holidays Jasmine tried to concentrate on her school-work, but every day was torture. Since the party, no one dared to make friends with Jasmine for fear of Maxine's wrath. In the playground they gave her a wide berth and only nodded a brief hello when she arrived at school or walked into the classroom. The teachers didn't seem to be aware of what was going on. All they were interested in were results.

It had been four months now since Jasmine had arrived in Barbados, but instead of things getting better, as her parents kept telling her they would, they were going from bad to worse. It all came to a head one evening when Jasmine was waiting for the bus.

The bus stop was teeming with pupils and, as usual, Jasmine kept her distance and stood in the shade until she heard the bus approaching. Nearby stood a First Year whose name was Giselle Forbes. She was a small, very skinny, mouse-like girl, who tended to keep herself to herself most of the time.

Without warning, two girls, also First Years, sidled up to her and one of them said something nasty.

Jasmine could see what was going on and how upset Giselle was. Without thinking, she walked over and stood next to her, placing her body between her and her two tormentors. 'Leave her alone,' said Jasmine.

'Hey, English Girl, why don't you mind you own business?'

'This is my business, so leave her alone.'

'Oh, are you going to make us, English?'

The bigger of the two came right up to Jasmine and stared into her face. 'Go back to where you come from,' she spat.

Jasmine's anger and frustration erupted, and before she could control herself she shoved the girl hard in the chest with both hands.

A look of surprise flickered across the girl's face as she staggered backwards over the uneven ground. Her heel caught an exposed root and she fell sprawling in a cloud of dust.

There was a loud gasp from everyone watching. Fighting outside school was just not done. Suddenly the crowd dispersed like magic. People just disappeared in a split second. Jasmine looked up and saw the reason why. Standing a few feet away was Mrs Dalgleish.

'Get up, Robinson, go and clean yourself up,' she said to the First Year girl. 'As for you, Jasmine Braithwaite, I am shocked and ashamed of you, brawling in the street in the uniform of Whittington School.'

'But... but I was defending...'

'I'm not interested in your excuses, young lady. I will see you in the morning.'

With that she marched off, leaving Jasmine standing alone, while everyone else stood a safe distance from her, sniggering with delight.

Jasmine said nothing to her parents that night but she hardly slept, thinking about the injustice, and going over and over what she was going to tell Mrs Dalgleish in the morning. Finally she fell into a fitful sleep which seemed to last only a few moments before her alarm clock shocked her into wakefulness.

She instantly thought about her meeting with Mrs Dalgleish. She got up, washed and ate her breakfast mechanically. As usual her mother was too busy to notice any difference in her behaviour.

When she arrived at school she noticed the others

in small groups glancing at her briefly, before turning away and whispering to each other. Then the bell went and everyone drifted into assembly.

Mrs Dalgleish was seated on the stage with all the other teachers, as usual, and when Jasmine went in and sat with her class her expression didn't change. She just stared straight ahead as she always did.

For a moment Jasmine hoped she had forgotten the incident, but unfortunately that was wishful thinking.

After Dr Mortimer had taken morning prayers he nodded at her class teacher. 'Last evening Mrs Dalgliesh witnessed a Whittington girl bringing the school into disgrace and disrepute by brawling in the street.' He paused for dramatic effect as the assembly sat waiting, with bated breath. 'The girl in question knows who she is. Will she please come forward, now.'

Jasmine sat transfixed, and just the occasional cough interrupted the deathly silence.

'I'm waiting,' said Dr Mortimer with exaggerated patience.

Jasmine got to her feet. All heads turned towards her and a ripple of hushed sniggering swept the room.

Her footsteps on the hardwood floor echoed loudly as she made her way to the front.

'Good. Now please turn and tell everyone your name.'

Jasmine turned to face the entire assembly, her knees trembling.

'My name is Jasmine Braithwaite,' she whispered.

'Louder please,' came the voice of Dr Mortimer.

'My name is Jasmine Braithwaite,' she repeated in a louder voice.

'Thank you, Miss Braithwaite. Please go and wait outside my office.'

Jasmine turned and walked slowly out of the hall, feeling every eye on her as she went.

She sat on the hard chair outside the Principal's office. She felt like an exhibit on show. The whole school trouped past the office, which was situated in the main corridor leading from the assembly hall.

Dr Mortimer came out with Mrs Dalgleish and stood at the entrance to the hall, talking and occasionally glancing in her direction. Eventually they parted and Dr Mortimer walked purposefully towards his office.

'Inside please, Miss Braithwaite,' he said firmly.

Jasmine remembered her last visit to his office, protected by her parents. This time she felt alone, afraid and vulnerable. But she tried hard not show it as she dug her nails hard into the palms of her hands.

Dr Mortimer paced up and down behind his desk before turning his back and looking out of the window. 'Jasmine Braithwaite, you have brought nothing but trouble with you since you came to this school. I was appalled by what Mrs Dalgleish told me she saw. Your parents came to the school complaining you were the victim of bullying, and yet I now find that you have been picking on a younger girl.'

'I wasn't picking on anybody. I was defen...'

'I am not interested in your excuses. Mrs Dalgliesh told me exactly what she saw and that's all I need to know.'

Jasmine wanted to scream out loud at the injustice, but instead she just dug her nails even harder into the palms of her hands.

Dr Mortimer continued. 'Your behaviour might be tolerated back in England but I can assure you it will not be allowed here. Under normal circumstances a pupil involved in such disgraceful behaviour would receive corporal punishment, but on this occasion you will only receive a warning. And let this be the last time I see you in my office. Is that clear?'

'Yes, sir,' muttered Jasmine.

'Now go back to your class.'

Jasmine quickly turned and, before the tears could burst from her eyes, she opened the door and fled into the corridor, shaking with anger and frustration. She felt utterly humiliated. She wanted to die there and then. She felt that her life couldn't get any worse - everything was going wrong.

She stopped for a while and leant against the wall outside her classroom. It took all her strength to gather her courage to enter the room.

'Go and sit down, Jasmine Braithwaite, and take out your history book. Now where were we?' Mrs Dalgleish said to the class, who, although desperate to stare at Jasmine, refrained from doing so for fear of the teacher's anger.

Jasmine couldn't concentrate. Her ears were full of the rushing sound of her angry blood pounding through her veins. She wasn't sure how much longer she could stand this living hell.

Chapter Twenty-three

Freedom had been taking on water now for a week or so, and the cracks in the hull were getting worse every time Luther took her out.

This was worrying, because each year all fishing boats in Barbados had to be inspected to get a certificate from the Ministry of Agriculture. If the boat didn't pass, then that was it! No certificate, no fishing... no money.

Reluctantly Luther had to face the prospect of getting *Freedom* out of the water and repairing the hull properly, even though it was an expensive, time-consuming and difficult operation.

The thought of this caused Luther to become more and more bad-tempered, and Devlin kept away from him as much as he could. Luther had also recently started drinking too much rum and usually by nine o'clock in the evening he was pretty much out of it. On several occasions Devlin had to help him to bed and leave him snoring, fully clothed, until he awoke the next morning with a hangover.

Eventually the inevitable happened. *Freedom* was lifted out of the water and placed up on the beach for repairs. The mobile crane arrived first thing in the morning, and the contractor proceeded to place two thick slings underneath the hull and attach them to the chain dangling from the arm of the crane.

Luther watched anxiously as the chain became taut, and his beloved boat slowly emerged from the water. Its green, barnacled hull dripped like a waterfall on to the stony beach, where a number of thick wooden logs were placed around the hull to prop her up.

Luther begrudgingly paid the crane-driver cash, and arranged for him to return the following week to put the boat back into the water when the repairs had been completed. 'We got a lot of work to do on the old girl,' he said, scratching his stubbly chin.

'But Dad, I've got exams coming up at school. I've got to study,' exclaimed Devlin, dismayed.

'Oh, so you won't help me, is that what you're saying? When I was your age I was helping my father with this boat. We used to bring in the biggest catches of all. Some day you will have your own boat, hopefully bigger and better than this.' He slapped his hand hard against the still-dripping side of *Freedom*. 'And your son will help you. Now, come on, there's work to do.'

Devlin sighed. He still couldn't seem to get his dad to understand that he had different plans. 'Dad,' he said calmly. 'We've been through this dozens of times. I want to go to university and study Fisheries Management.'

'What the heck is that all about? I've taught you all you need to know about fishing. What do those professors up at Cave Hill University know, that I don't?'

Devlin knew it was pointless to argue. His dad was set in his ways and all he had ever known was fishing.

❖ ❖ ❖

Jasmine had slept late, and when she padded into the kitchen she was surprised to see Dad. He had come over unexpectedly, and seemed to have something on his mind, as he sat talking to Grannie Brathwaite in hushed tones on her veranda.

'Hello, Dad.'

'Hi, Jazzie,' said her dad. 'I'm just chatting with

your grannie. I won't be a minute.'

Jasmine shrugged and went back into the kitchen to look for something to eat.

The window was ajar and she could hear her dad's voice. He sounded tense and worried, and every now and then Grannie Braithwaite would interject with an 'Eh eh!' or an 'Oh gawd, oh gawd'.

Jasmine moved closer to the window and pushed it a little wider open.

'I don't know where to turn, Mum. The guys just don't want to work and now Mr O'Brien is charging me penalties for being over schedule. At this rate I'll be broke in a month. I don't want us to sell Summerland House to that crook Harrison, but we might have to.'

'No, son, you've got to stand up to him. The house has been in our family for generations and when I die you can carry on the tradition. If you sell to Harrison he'll just put up some of those dreadful flats and another piece of Bajan history will disappear.'

'I know, Mum. Marcia and I came back to Barbados to make a good life for ourselves. We just want the best for Jasmine and for her to be happy. She's all we've got. But it's not working out the way we wanted.'

'Don't give up, son, just have faith and believe.

246

Things will work out.'

'I hope so, Mum, I hope so.'

Jasmine backed away from the window. If they wanted me to be happy so much, why did they bring me out here? she thought.

❖ ❖ ❖

Later that day Jasmine met Devlin at the bus stop. They had arranged to go into Bridgetown, and Devlin was going to reveal his plan for her escape.

On the journey, Devlin was quieter than usual. He sat staring out of the window.

'What's up?' said Jasmine. 'You seem far away.'

'It's my dad. He just doesn't understand that I don't want to spend my life as a fisherman. I want to go to university, I want to see the world.'

'Come back to England with me,' said Jasmine.

'Maybe I will,' said Devlin thoughtfully.

They got off the bus just before the main town and headed towards the docks. They were surrounded by high fences, behind which were stacked rows of brightly coloured metal containers.

At the quaysides there were dozens of cargo ships, and towering above everything were two huge cruise ships, which were being prepared to take thousands of passengers round the Caribbean.

Devlin had arranged with his uncle Norris to pick up two passes from the security guard at the gate. The guard on duty knew Devlin and handed him the plastic visitor cards with a smile. 'Hey, is this your girlfriend?'

Devlin looked embarrassed. 'She's my friend,' he muttered.

'Say hello to Norris for me,' the guard said, winking at Devlin.

'I will,' said Devlin. 'Oh, by the way, where's the *Avlis* being loaded?'

The guard looked at his sheet. '*Avlis*… ah, here we go, *MV Avlis*, she's at Dock Seventeen.'

They strolled along the road which skirted the vast areas where cranes busily loaded and unloaded containers. Devlin seemed to know exactly where he was going, and very soon they were heading towards a less busy part of the docks.

The ships at this quayside were smaller, and instead of cranes and containers, fork-lift trucks loaded smaller crates on to pallets, which were then lifted by the ship's own crane into the cavernous hold.

Eventually Devlin stopped and pointed at one of the ships. 'This is the *Avlis*,' he said with a business-like note in his voice. 'It's going to the UK loaded with sugar. It leaves next week.'

Jasmine felt a thrill of excitement run through her. She looked at the gangplank leading up to the deck. At the top, two sailors were leaning on the rail, smoking and laughing loudly.

'Is that where I get on the ship?'

'No, security is too tight to get on board here,' he said, his eyes scanning the ship. 'We have to wait till she's ready to leave. She will wait for the port pilot to lead her out. That's when we get on board.'

Jasmine was astonished at how cool Devlin was about the escape plan. He wasn't at all nervous and seemed to have everything planned.

'So this time next week you will be on your way back to England,' he said in a matter-of-fact way. With that, he turned and walked back towards the exit.

Jasmine was speechless. Could it be that easy? Her mind raced with thoughts of going back to England and feeling as if she belonged.

'Come on Jazzie, let's go,' called Devlin.

Jasmine followed him, glancing back over her shoulder at the ship that was her passport to freedom.

She thought of nothing else over the weekend. Soon she would be leaving Barbados behind, and this thought gave her the strength and confidence to feel that she could cope with anything.

❖ ❖ ❖

Jasmine started counting down the days as they crawled slowly by. At last there were only five days to go until her great escape.

That day she felt particularly confident, and she arrived at school early. Instead of going to her usual hiding-place under the tree, she waited by the gateway where Maxine and her gang usually stood. She took a deep breath and waited for everyone to arrive.

She watched a dozen or so First Years get off the bus. They gawped at her apprehensively as they went in, keeping their distance. Gradually the playground filled up, and several cars arrived and dropped people off in twos and threes. She noticed people nudging each other when they saw her standing in Maxine's territory, but no one said anything.

Eventually Maxine came walking up the road.

She spotted Jasmine immediately and headed straight for her. At the same time, Josie and Suzanne arrived on the next bus, and they joined Maxine as she sauntered towards the school gate.

As they crossed the threshold Maxine opened her mouth to speak, but before she could do so, Jasmine spoke in a loud voice.

'Your parents decided which of them is going to be stuck with you yet, Maxine? You must be worried your dad will get you. Then you'll have an English step-mum. You might even have to go and live in England.'

Everyone in the area stopped talking.

Maxine was struck dumb for a moment but quickly found her voice. 'What's got into you, Braithwaite? Why don't you go and hide under your tree?'

'I think I'll stay right here. I quite like it.'

Maxine was clearly rattled at having her little patch of territory invaded by Jasmine.

Jasmine went on. 'What's it like not knowing who you will end up with? Does it make you hate everyone? Does it make you want to hurt others the way you hurt inside?'

Maxine's face twitched at Jasmine's words, but Jasmine continued. 'Does it make you want to bully people and make their lives as miserable as yours? It's not your fault your parents screwed up, so don't take it out on other people. Look around you, Maxine. Nobody here likes you, because you're a bully. It's about time we all stood up to you. You ruin people's lives, because your life is a mess.'

Maxine's bottom lip was beginning to quiver at Jasmine's onslaught. For once in her life she was the one everyone was staring at, the one being humiliated.

'Come on. Anybody here like Maxine?' shouted Jasmine. 'Raise your hand.'

Josie and Suzanne looked at each other, each waiting to see if the other would raise her hand, but neither of them did.

Maxine stared at them venomously. 'You're supposed to be my friends!' she screamed, looking round at everyone.

All around the playground there was not one single hand raised aloft.

'You see, Maxine, no one likes a bully. You can't frighten people into liking you. You have to earn respect and friendship.'

Slowly, everyone turned away from Maxine and walked over to Jasmine and stood by her.

It was the final straw. Maxine's face contorted into a mask of anguish. Tears burst from her eyes and huge sobs shook her body. 'My parents do love me,' she sobbed. 'They do....' Her voice trailed off into a whimper.

Jasmine walked over to Maxine, clasped her shoulders tightly with both hands and stared deeply into her tearful eyes. 'It's not your fault. Just because you're a victim, don't make victims out of us.' Then she walked away. And Suzanne, Josie, Breezy and Broderick tucked in behind her.

'You were great, Jasmine, can we hang out with you?' said Breezy.

'I don't need friends like you,' said Jasmine, with a note of satisfaction in her voice.

❖ ❖ ❖

When she met up with Devlin that afternoon, she told him what had happened.

'Hey, that's great,' said Devlin. 'She sounds like she needed someone to stand up to her.'

'I didn't like making her cry, though. I felt sorry for her. She looked so pathetic.'

'Bullies are pathetic and I've met a few,' he said.

They walked the rest of the way in silence until they reached the top of the hill and arrived outside the tiny store, which sold everything: fruit, newspapers, chocolate, tools, even live chickens.

'I gotta get my dad's newspaper and Lotto ticket,' said Devlin.

They stepped into the dark, cluttered shop. Shafts of sunlight from the numerous cracks between its planked walls pierced the gloom. Behind the counter sat an ancient old man, who barely moved as they approached.

'Usual please, Joseph,' said Devlin.

The old man handed over the ticket and newspaper without a word.

'He doesn't say much,' said Jasmine as they stepped out into the sunlight.

'Well, he's ninety-two years old. My dad says he's said all he's got to say.'

When they reached Grannie Braithwaite's, Devlin turned and looked at Jasmine intently. 'Are you sure you want to go through with it?' he said, staring deep into her eyes.

Jasmine had no hesitation. 'Yes, I'm sure,' she said firmly.

'OK then, I'll see you on the beach on Saturday at three. Don't be late. The *Avlis* will leave on time and we can't miss it.'

'I'll be there,' said Jasmine.

Chapter Twenty-four

Two days before Jasmine was due to leave, something happened that convinced her even more that her decision to escape was right.

She was sitting at the computer, in a small study just off the living room. She was alternating between playing a game and half-heartedly writing an essay which was supposed to be delivered the next day. The essay didn't matter, of course, because she wouldn't be at school to see what mark it got. She would be on the open sea, heading for England.

Dad was out on the veranda, working on some figures, and Mum was watching the news on TV.

All of a sudden Mum let out a yell. 'Dave, Dave, come and look. There's something about Carlton Harrison on the news!'

'Quick, turn it up,' said Dave, rushing into the room.

Jasmine joined her parents as a picture of Harrison flashed up on the screen. The newsreader announced:

'Financier and property developer Carlton Harrison was arrested in a dawn raid by Drug Squad officers at his luxury home this morning! The arrest followed an undercover surveillance operation led by Chief Inspector Alleyne of the Barbados police. Mr Harrison's high-powered speedboat, the Barracuda, was impounded as it unloaded a consignment of drugs in a secluded bay on the East coast of the island late last night.'

'I knew he was a crook!' shouted Dave.

'Ssshh, Dave, look, there's Chief Inspector Alleyne.'

'Following a tip-off, my team of officers waited for the Barracuda in Craggy Bay where other members of the gang were waiting to unload the drugs. That's all I can say at the moment. Thank you.'

'A tip-off. I wonder who it was?' said Marcia.

Jasmine just smiled to herself.

The newsreader continued: 'Four men were arrested at the scene and are in police custody.'

Four mug-shot photos came up on the screen.

'My God, look!' exclaimed Dave.

'What is it?' asked Marcia.

'It's Vince, my foreman! I don't believe it... I suspected he was working for Harrison, but this is incredible.'

'Do you realise what this means, Dave?' said Mum. 'We don't have to sell!' She hugged him joyfully. 'You can tell O'Brien that it was Harrison all along, paying Vince to hold things up. I'm sure he'll be more understanding now.'

'Yes, you're right. O'Brien's a good man, and he'll have lots more work for me after I finish this job.'

Jasmine's heart sank. This meant they would definitely be staying in Barbados. There was now no chance of them ever moving back to England. Devlin's escape plan was her only hope.

This time there would be no mistakes. She had been preparing carefully for the journey. The stupid escapade in London and the pathetic attempt at sailing home had taught her valuable lessons. No, this time it would be different.

Every day she had sneaked a piece of clothing out of the house in her school bag, and each evening at Grannie Braithwaite's she had transferred it into a strong rucksack. Other necessary items were also in there: a torch, biscuits, cereal bars, sweets and crisps, as well as small tins of food for the two-week journey. She even had some English money she had kept in her purse - about forty pounds, which should be enough to get her to London from Southampton.

Jasmine planned to stay at Grannie Braithwaite's for the weekend, and her parents happily agreed. They were glad to get some time to themselves after the good news.

On the last morning of Jasmine's time in Barbados the sun rose as usual above the blue Caribbean sea. Jasmine looked out of her bedroom window, knowing that soon she would be heading away from Barbados and all the unhappiness she had found there. She got ready, dressed herself and made one final check of her rucksack, making sure everything was in there for her journey.

Breakfast was always special at Grannie Braithwaite's: slices of Bajan ham, scrambled eggs and thick slices of soft, home-baked bread.

'You seem far away, Jasmine,' smiled Grannie Braithwaite.

'I'm fine,' said Jasmine quickly.

Grannie Braithwaite looked at her through narrowed eyes. 'Are you sure, darlin'? I can sense there's somethin' not right about you today.'

'No, really, I'm fine.'

'What's in that big bag? It looks very heavy.'

'Oh, it's sports gear. You know, hockey stuff. I'm the goal-keeper, we've got a game this afternoon.'

'I'm worried about you, young lady,' said Grannie Braithwaite, looking hard at Jasmine. 'That's what you are now, a young lady, and you have to start thinking about the future and what you're going to do with your life. So don't do anything you might regret,' she finished, with a note of worry in her voice.

'I won't, Grannie B,' said Jasmine, feeling a little guilty. She didn't like lying to her grandmother.

That day, time seemed to drag. Each hour, minute and second ticked by excruciatingly slowly. To keep her mind occupied, she helped to clear the table, washed the dishes and dusted around. At about two-thirty, she picked up her rucksack and called out to Grannie Braithwaite that she was off to the hockey match.

'Have a good match, darlin',' said Grannie Braithwaite, coming out to see her off.

'I will,' said Jasmine. Suddenly something stirred inside her. She dropped her bag and threw her arms round Grannie Braithwaite, kissing and hugging her tightly.

'Eh eh, what's all this? You actin' as if you're not goin' to see me again.'

Jasmine bit hard on her lip. How she would miss Grannie Braithwaite, who somehow connected with her emotionally and understood her inner thoughts.

But that wasn't enough to keep her here. Purposefully, she picked up her bag and walked quickly down the wooden steps on to the road with tears in her eyes. She dared not look back.

Somehow, leaving Grannie Braithwaite was even harder than leaving her parents. She loved them, but they just didn't understand how unhappy their actions had made her. Now all she wanted was to get out of Barbados, where she had almost drowned in a sea of tears.

She walked determinedly towards the beach, to where she had arranged to meet Devlin. The plan was simple. They were to take his dad's small motor boat and head back along the coast to the port, where the fully-loaded *Avlis* would be lying at anchor, waiting for the pilot to take her out beyond the reef.

Chapter Twenty-five

That morning Devlin had been up for two hours, getting on with some chores and cleaning up the kitchen before Luther finally woke up.

'Mornin', boy,' said Luther, holding his hand over his eyes. 'I think I had a bit too much rum last night.'

'I just made some coffee,' said Devlin, nodding in the direction of the table.

'I hope you're going to help me with the caulking today. There's still a whole load of gaps to fill in the hull before we paint her.'

Caulking was a filthy job and Devlin hated it. It involved filling the gaps between the planks of *Freedom's* hull with a thick, black, tar-like material to stop the water getting in. But the worst part was getting the old caulking out first. This was done by heating it up with a blowtorch and digging the softened goo out of the cracks.

It was smelly and hot work, but it had to be done. Only older boats like *Freedom* were made from wood.

The modern ones were fibre-glass or steel. But they were very expensive, as Luther kept reminding Devlin whenever he complained about all the maintenance they had to do on *Freedom*.

Half an hour later Devlin and Luther made their way across the road and down the beach to the area where *Freedom* was lying. There were two or three old hulks rotting away under the trees, and piles of old wood and rusty parts from long-dead fishing boats. An old car, its engine gone, stood on piles of bricks instead of wheels.

Luther unlocked the padlock on the small shed and took out the tools. He handed Devlin an old scraper and a battered blowtorch. 'You do that bit.' He pointed to a patch of bare wooden planking. 'I'll do the waterline.' And without another word he lit the gas flame of his own blowtorch and climbed the rickety ladder which leaned against the hull.

Devlin sulkily got on with heating up the old filler until it was soft, then digging it out and scraping it clear. The acrid smoke made his eyes water and the heat caused the sweat to run down his back.

The time dragged by and every now and then he glanced at his watch. He knew Jasmine would be meeting him further up the beach in a few hours and he wanted to get as much done as possible before he told his dad he was leaving. So he worked as hard and as quickly as he could. He slaved away diligently all morning without even a break for lunch, but kept a close eye on the time.

'Why you keep lookin' at you watch, boy?' shouted Luther from his ladder. 'You got some place to be?'

'Maybe,' said Devlin.

'You ain't goin nowhere. We gotta finish this boat so we can get her certified.'

'This boat's a wreck,' flared Devlin. 'We're wasting our time filling up the cracks with this gunk. I'm fed up with all this hard work. It's pointless. Anyway, I'm meeting someone this afternoon so you'll have to manage without me.'

'Who you meetin'? That girl, I bet. She's nothin' but trouble. I'm tellin' you to keep away from her. I forbid you to see her, y'hear me, boy?'

'Don't keep calling me boy!' Devlin's temper was starting to get the better of him now. He'd never answered his dad back before, but now he'd just had enough of being told who he could talk to and what he could and couldn't do. 'You can't stop me from seeing who I want to see.'

Luther got down the ladder and put down his

blowtorch. He stood threateningly over Devlin. 'Don't you talk to me like that, boy. You do as you're told. And I'm tellin' you, you're not goin' anywhere. So get on with your work.'

Something snapped inside Devlin. He slowly put down his scraper and turned off his blowtorch. Then he stood up and faced his father. They were almost the same height, although Luther was a lot heavier. 'I'm not a boy and you can't tell me what to do any more.'

Luther's eyes widened with surprise, but before he could answer, Devlin stepped sideways and shouldered his way past, almost knocking his father over.

For a second or two Luther was stunned into silence, Before he could react, Devlin had snatched up his rucksack and was halfway up the beach. Without looking back, he broke into a fast run.

'You come back here, boy!' Luther roared. 'Devlin... come back here at once....'

But Devlin was already out of earshot and Luther knew he stood no chance of catching him. He looked around at *Freedom* and suddenly the truth of what Devlin had said hit him. She was a wreck and no amount of work was going to keep her going much longer.

His shoulders hunched and he pounded the side of the boat with his fists. Then his body sagged, and he slid down the side of the boat and sat with his head bowed between his knees. On the tree-stump in front of him sat a half-finished bottle of rum. He reached out and removed the cork, and took a long swig.

❖ ❖ ❖

Further along the beach, near the place where all the fishing boats were moored, Jasmine sat nervously waiting for Devlin. He was ten minutes late and she was beginning to get anxious. Nearby, pulled up on the beach was Luther's small dinghy which was used to get across to *Freedom* when she was in the water. It was as old as *Freedom* and just as decrepid. The ancient outboard motor was rusty and battered, but thanks to constant maintenance it still managed to work.

At last, to Jasmine's relief, Devlin came running along the beach. She stood up and waved. Devlin waved back and slowed to a walk.

'I thought you weren't coming after all,' she said.

Devlin said nothing. He sat down, his back against the dinghy. He was panting, and sweat ran in little rivulets down his forehead into his eyes. He wiped them away with the back of his hand.

Jasmine watched him for a moment. 'Are you OK?' she said tentatively.

'I had a fight with my dad. I pushed him out of the way,' said Devlin, shaking his bowed head.

'Oh, Dev,' she gasped. 'It's my fault, I shouldn't have asked you to help me.'

'No, it's not your fault. He's had it coming for ages. He's always putting me down. He treats me like a slave. I hate him.'

'Don't say that, Dev, it's not true.'

Devlin said nothing. He got to his feet and looked out towards the sea, shielding his eyes from the sun. In the distance he could make out a line of ships anchored about a kilometre up the coast. One of them was the *Avlis*, its distinctive red hull standing out in the afternoon sunlight.

'C'mon,' he said. 'She'll be leaving once she's fuelled up.' He picked up their bags and put them into the dinghy. Then he pushed the little craft down the beach to the water's edge. 'Get in and sit in the front.'

Jasmine gingerly stepped into the boat, Devlin gave one more shove and the boat floated into the lapping waves. He continued to push until the water came up to his knees, then he expertly got in and pulled the starter cord. The outboard motor clattered noisily to life in a cloud of acrid smoke.

Devlin settled down beside it and silently steered the tiny boat towards the waiting ship.

Jasmine was nervous and desperately tried to think of something to say. 'Did you hear about that crook Carlton Harrison getting arrested?' she asked.

'Yeah, that'll wipe the sneer off Ronnie's face,' Devlin said with a note of satisfaction in his voice. 'It turns out his dad's a drug-runner.'

'At least your dad's an honest fisherman,' Jasmine said.

Devlin nodded. He'd never thought about it like that. 'Yeah, I guess you're right,' he said thoughtfully.

Silence fell upon them again.

Even though the sea looked calm, it rocked the tiny boat violently as it butted its way through the waves towards the *Avlis*. As they drew closer, Devlin shut the motor down and let the dinghy float silently right up to the towering side of the ship.

'The ladder's on the other side,' he whispered. 'It's there for the pilot to get on board and take the ship out, so most of the crew will be below until he arrives. We've got to get round there without being seen.'

Devlin edged the dinghy silently along the side of the ship with his hands until it passed under the anchor chain at the front, and then back along the other side to where the pilot's ladder hung. It was made of two strands of thick rope, with wooden rungs every eighteen inches. It was the final challenge that stood in the way of Jasmine's escape.

'Well, Jazzie, this is it,' breathed Devlin. 'Once you're on board, find a hiding-place and stay there.'

Jasmine was confused. 'I thought you were coming with me!' she said.

Devlin didn't answer. He just looked up at the ladder, then back at the thin strip of white sand with low rolling hills behind it. His mind was racing, his emotions torn.

Finally he said quietly, 'Barbados is my home. Like you said, I was born here. I'm the son of an honest fisherman. I have to go back and face him and make the best of it. You'll be all right without me. Now go, we don't have time to waste.'

Jasmine's stomach turned over and she felt sick. She wasn't sure whether it was because of the rocking boat, or because she was about to climb that rickety rope ladder alone, without her protector, Devlin, and stow away on a ship back to England.

Whatever it was, she hesitated and looked at Devlin anxiously.

Suddenly, she thought of her parents, the sacrifices they had made and the pressures they were under. Her Grandma's parting words came back to her. She was a young lady now and had to make the right decisions.

In that instant she realised how stupid and selfish she was being, and understood that running away was not going to solve things. Anyway, Devlin was going to need a friend, and she was the only one he had.

'Take me back, Devlin, I don't want to go to England. I'm going to stick it out, and like you say, make the best of it.'

Devlin looked at her intently. 'Are you sure that's what you want?'

'Yes,' she nodded. 'I'm very sure!'

Then his face broke into a smile. He pulled the

starting cord and the old engine coughed back into life. 'Barbados, here we come,' he laughed, as he opened the throttle and pointed the bow back towards the island he called home.

Chapter Twenty-six

The sun was dropping towards the horizon in another magical display of orange and pink by the time they got back to the beach and pulled the dinghy on to dry land.

Devlin stood looking at Jasmine, not knowing what to say. All he knew was that he had to go home and face Luther, something he wasn't looking forward to.

Jasmine instinctively knew she couldn't leave him. 'Let me come home with you. If I'm there it might help.'

Devlin nodded. 'Thanks,' he said.

They set off along the beach and, without thinking, Jasmine put her hand in his.

The rocky beach arced round to the right, past the road, then up towards the fishing village where Devlin's house was. Most of the smaller fishing boats had already been pulled up on to the beach. Beyond them was the place where Devlin had left Luther earlier and where *Freedom* lay on her wooden props.

But even before they reached the point where they would see *Freedom* Devlin knew something was not right.

A flickering orange light appeared above the clump of palm trees that hung over the beach. The normally clear air had a faint tinge of something acrid and the sound of raised voices drifted towards them. As they approached the last hillock of sand and rock before the village came into view Devlin's pace quickened. Something was wrong, very wrong.

His walk turned into a run and Jasmine struggled to keep up with her heavy rucksack. He reached the promontory before her and what he saw froze him in mid step. The beach and the village beyond was lit by a red glow, and a pall of thick black smoke drifted out to sea.

Jasmine caught up and grabbed Devlin's arm. 'Oh my God,' she screamed.

Freedom was engulfed in flames from end to end. They licked and curled greedily round the curves of her hull. Spitting and flaring, they devoured her. They leaped as high as the palm trees, like demons dancing on the beach. All around, dark figures seemed to dance with the flames in a kind of ritual ceremony.

It was only when one of them ran down the beach carrying a plastic bucket did it become clear that they were local men trying to douse the flames. But their efforts were futile and they drew back from the intense heat in defeat.

Devlin sprinted the last twenty metres, shouting incoherently. He snatched a bucket out of the hands of one of the men who stood watching her burn. He threw the water at the flames, but it just evaporated in a pathetic hiss of steam.

The man grabbed him and pulled him away. 'It's no use, Dev!' he yelled over the crackling flames. 'It's too late, she's a gonner.'

'Where's my dad?' Devlin looked frantically round at the ten or so sweaty, orange, glistening faces.

They all looked at each other, realising simultaneously that Luther was not amongst them. No one spoke. Each man had the same thought. If Luther had been on board *Freedom* when she went up, there was little chance he would have been able to get out in time.

Devlin threw the bucket down and ran up the beach towards the road.

Without hesitating, Jasmine sprinted after him.

Devlin's house was set a hundred yards back behind the road, on the other side of the community hall, which blocked it from view. Devlin skidded round the corner and up the path which led to the front door. He fumbled desperately in his jeans pocket for his key.

Jasmine arrived and stood watching anxiously. The lights were on and Jasmine thought she hear something. 'Ssshhh,' she said. 'What's that noise?'

Devlin stopped and listened at the door.

Above the chorus of the frogs and insects they could hear the sound of hysterical laughter, interspersed with the occasional yell, accompanied by loud banging. In the background the television was on and the newsreader's voice mingled confusingly with the other sounds from inside the house.

'It's my dad,' said Devlin, breathing a sigh of relief. 'He's alive.'

'But he sounds as if he's gone crazy,' said Jasmine, with a worried look on her face.

Devlin finally found his key and held it up. 'We've got to go in and find out,' he said. He put the key into the lock, turned it and cautiously pushed open the door.

Luther was standing in front of the blaring TV

with his back to the door. In his left hand he held a small white piece of paper which he waved about frantically, while his right hand banged the table so hard the cups and plates on it jumped up and down.

'Dad, are you all right?' yelled Devlin over the noise.

Luther spun round. His face was contorted into a grin and tears ran down his cheeks. When he saw Devlin he grabbed the remote and turned the TV down. 'Devlin boy, I've been waiting for you.'

These were the words Devlin had been dreading. His dad wasn't going to forget his earlier behaviour and now there was going to be an almighty row.

Luther noticed Jasmine standing in the doorway. 'Oh, it's you, girl, come in, come in.'

Jasmine hesitated. Maybe she shouldn't get involved. But Luther walked past her to the door and pushed it closed. 'Well, you really did it this time, boy,' he said.

'I'm sorry, Dad,' said Devlin quietly.

'Sorry! Sorry?' Luther bellowed. 'Why would you be sorry?'

Devlin and Jasmine looked at each other in puzzlement.

'You did it, boy, you did it... Look.' He shook the

piece of paper in Devlin's face.

Devlin was convinced his dad had gone stark, raving mad. 'What, what have I done?'

'What have you done? You've won us the Lotto, all the numbers. We've won the jackpot, we're rich....!' yelled Luther.

Before Jasmine and Devlin could speak, the door burst open and Frank, one of the fishermen who had been fighting the blaze, came running in.

'Luther, thank Gawd you're alive,' he exclaimed joyfully.

Luther looked puzzled. 'Of course I'm alive. A little worse for wear,' he said, picking up the empty rum bottle. 'But alive!'

'Dad.... I don't know how to tell you this, but there's been a fire,' said Devlin cautiously. '*Freedom*... she's burnt out....'

'We think someone left a blowtorch on underneath her,' interrupted Frank. 'She was well alight before the alarm was raised.'

Luther looked guilty. 'Well, I guess that was me,' he said, looking at the rum bottle again. 'After you went, Devlin, I just looked at her and I realised that what you were saying was true. So I tried to find comfort in the bottom of this bottle. I know it's not the answer, but I came back here and finished it off. Then I must have fallen asleep. I only woke up ten minutes ago and switched on the TV to check the Lotto numbers, and found out we won.'

'You've won the lottery!' shouted Frank excitedly. 'Well, I guess you won't be needing your boat any longer, you can live a life of ease.... No more fishing for you, eh?'

Luther looked surprised. 'No more fishing? Are you crazy, man? I can afford a new fifty-footer now, and a full-time crew. So you and the rest of the guys better watch out for *Freedom the Second*! And as for you, Devlin boy, I think you should get down to some serious studying if you're going to get into that university.'

Devlin and Jasmine looked at each other, their eyes bright as moonbeams. What a day it had been.

'I'm so glad I didn't climb that ladder,' said Jasmine.

'Me too,' said Devlin.

'I'd better go now,' said Jasmine. 'Grannie B will be getting worried about me. She thinks I'm playing hockey.'

'Come on, I'll walk you home before the news

spreads and everyone comes over to celebrate,' said Devlin, 'At least I don't have to be up early in the morning for fishing.' He grinned.

The light on Grannie Braithwaite's porch was burning brightly and dozens of moths were circling it. Grannie B was sitting in her usual chair, rocking steadily back and forth.

As they came up the wooden steps she greeted them with a smile. 'Hello, you two. I didn't think you were coming back, Jasmine. I thought you might be trying to go back to England again.' She winked mischievously. 'How did the hockey match go?'

Jasmine looked flustered. 'Er, er...'

'It was called off,' interrupted Devlin. 'So we went for a ride in my dad's dinghy.'

Jasmine glanced at Devlin. He always came to her rescue. 'That's right, Grannie B, it's been quite an afternoon. I'll tell you all about it later.'

Devlin walked back down the steps and stood at the bottom.

Jasmine followed him. 'Thanks for everything today, Dev.'

'Oh, it was nothing.'

'I hope you're still going to talk to me now you're

a sqillioniare?' she smiled.

'I will, as long as you help me with my homework.'

Without warning he leant forward and kissed her on the cheek. 'See you soon,' he said as he turned. And for the first time, he trotted away without looking back, because he knew now she would always be there.

Jasmine smiled. She realised she had been blind. She did have a true friend here in Barbados, one she could rely on unconditionally. Her friendships back in London were beyond the sea of tears and maybe one day they would be revived... but that was in the future.

She went back up the steps, her hand touching her cheek.

'I knew you liked him,' chuckled Grannie Braithwaite.

Jasmine turned and looked out at the moon which reflected like a silver searchlight on the surface of the sea. 'It's so beautiful here, Grannie B,' she sighed.

At that moment Jasmine's parents drew up in

their car. 'Hi, Jazzie,' cried her mum. 'Did you have a nice day?'

'Oh yes,' said Jasmine. 'Unforgettable. How about you two?'

'Not bad,' said her dad, grinning. 'Come on, let's get you home where you belong.'

'Yes,' nodded Jasmine. 'Where I belong.'

SEA OF TEARS ACKNOWLEDGEMENTS

This is my first novel and there have been many people both in the UK and Barbados who have helped and advised me. They are:

Lawyer Peter Williams and Magistrate Faith Marshal-Harris, who advised on law and court procedure in Barbados.

Master Chief Petty Officer Leroy Stuart, HMBS Pelican, Barbados Coast Guard, whose enthusiasm for the book was inspiring.

PCs Kesha Greenidge and Ernest Mellows, at District ' D' Station in Holetown, Barbados, two fine Bajan police officers.

The staff of Port St Charles, Barbados, for allowing me access to their exclusive residential marina.

Bill Tinsley, ex-Metropolitan Police Royalty Protection Officer, for his expert knowledge on UK Police procedure.

Barnardo' s, NSPCC and CEOP for the incredible work they do with runaways and sexually exploited children and young people.

My friends Ken Follett and Julian Fellowes for their support and advice.

Jan & Ludo Marcelo, who brought the issue of Caribbean returnees to my attention.

Pam Janson-Smith, Patricia McLean and Alvina Benjamin-Taylor for their brilliant proofreading and gentle criticism.

Janetta Otter-Barry and the team at Frances Lincoln for their dedication to promoting cultural diversity.

And finally my husband Keith for his technical know-how and eye for detail. He is my rock and eternal supporter and without him this book would not have been written.

FLOELLA BENJAMIN OBE is an iconic children's television presenter, as well as a producer, actress and author, who for over 35 years has dedicated her life to making children happy and campaigning for their well-being. She has written over 20 books including *Skip Across the Ocean*, *My Two Grannies* and *My Two Grandads* for Frances Lincoln, as well as her acclaimed autobiography, *Coming To England*, of which the Daily Telegraph said, "Few other books are as enlightening – or as important – as this one." It was made into an award-winning film for the BBC in 2003. Also, *The Arms of Britannia*, an account of her teenage years in the 60s, was published in 2010. Floella received an OBE and a BAFTA Special Lifetime Award for her contribution to broadcasting. She is Chancellor of the University of Exeter, and in 2010 she was made a Life Peer, with the title Baroness Benjamin of Beckenham, Kent. She is married, with two children, and lives in south London.

FAR FROM HOME
Na'ima B Robert

Katie and Tariro are worlds apart but their lives are linked
by a terrible secret, gradually revealed in this compelling
story of two girls grappling with the complexities of
adolescence, family and a painful colonial legacy.
14-year-old Tariro loves her ancestral home, the baobab tree
she was born beneath, her loving family – and brave,
handsome Nhamo. She couldn't be happier.
But then the white settlers arrive and everything
changes – suddenly, violently and tragically.
Forty years later, 14-year-old Katie loves her
doting father, her exclusive boarding school
and her farm with its baobab tree in rural Zimbabwe.
Life is great. Until the family are forced to leave
everything and escape to cold, rainy London
Atmospheric, gripping and epic in scope, *Far From Home*
brings the turbulent history of Zimbabwe
to vivid, tangible life.

FROM SOMALIA WITH LOVE
Na'ima B. Robert

My name is Safia Dirie. My family has always been my mum,
Hoyo, and my two older brothers, Ahmed and Abdullahi.
I don't really remember Somalia – I'm an East London girl.
But now Abo, my father, is coming to live with us,
after twelve long years. How am I going to cope?

Safia knows that there will be changes ahead but nothing has
prepared her for the reality of dealing with Abo's cultural
expectations, her favourite brother Ahmed's wild ways, and
the temptation of her cousin Firdous' party-girl lifestyle.
Safia must come to terms with who she is – as a Muslim,
as a teenager, as a poet, as a friend, but most of all,
as a daughter to a father she has never known. Safia must
find her own place in the world, so both father and daughter
can start to build the relationship they long for.

From Somalia, with Love is one girl's quest to discover
who she is – a story rooted in Somali and Muslim life that
will strike a chord with young people everywhere.

BRAVE NEW GIRL
Catherine Johnson

Seren is full of brilliant ideas – it's just that she always seems to put her foot in it! First there was the dance routine where she fell off the stage. And now her plan to get her sister Sasha noticed by gorgeous Luke Beckford looks like it could backfire…. Seren reckons she's just hopelessly accident-prone! But there's one person who believes in Seren. Her mate Keith is making a film for a national competition and he wants Seren to be in it. Could Seren turn out to be a star after all? This is a funny, big-hearted story with a lovable heroine who will make you laugh and cry.

BLOOD RUNNER
James Riordan

"Not far now. His lungs are bursting, his legs are as heavy as rocks, his breath rasps in his throat. Every ounce of his body screams STOP! Yet his will is still strong. He has to make it. For his President. For the black people of South Africa. See, if I can do it, so can you!"

Samuel Gquibela's parents and sister die in a bloody massacre. His brothers retaliate by joining the anti-Apartheid movement, with guns and terrorism as their weapons. But Sam decides to fight prejudice in his own way, as a runner. Against all odds – from a poor township childhood to the Bantu homelands, from work in a gold-mine to competing for gold – he focuses his mind, body and heart on the long, hard race to freedom...